"I have no ring to give you."

"We don't need rings. I only want to love you."

Rose moved to Kathleen's side. "I'll marry you," she said, taking Kathleen's hand in her own. "I'll marry you for better or for worse, in sickness and in health, whether you're rich or poor. And I'll always honor and cherish you, Kathleen. Always." She looked at Kathleen with something very strong in her eyes.

Kathleen straightened her back and repeated Rose's words.

"I'll kiss you tonight, Kathleen, darling. I'll lie on top of you, head to toe. I'll tuck your head beneath me chin and hook me feet beneath yours. Me arms will be wrapped around you, and one hand will cradle your head against me. I'll love you forever, Kathleen, forever and ever."

Kathleen O'Donald

A NOVEL BY

PENNY HAYES

Kathleen O'Donald

A NOVEL BY

PENNY HAYES

The Naiad Press, Inc.
1994

Printed in the United States of America on acid-free paper
First Edition

Edited by Christine Cassidy
Cover design by Pat Tong and Bonnie Liss
    (Phoenix Graphics)
Typeset by Sandi Stancil

Library of Congress Cataloging-in-Publication Data

Hayes, Penny, 1940–
    Kathleen O'Donald / by Penny Hayes
        p.   cm.
    ISBN 1-56280-070-1
        1. Women clothing workers—New England—Fiction.   2.
Lesbians—New England—Fiction.   I. Title.
PS3558.A835K38   1994
813'.54—dc20   93-41451
                                                            CIP

*For their acts of bravery this story is
lovingly dedicated to:*

*My grandmother Marya Lipka
who came through Ellis Island in 1912,*

The women and men who died March 25, 1911,

Karen McGough, my wonderful partner

This is a story of fiction. The time is correct. There was a Triangle Shirtwaist Company now called the Brown Building, located on the corner of Greene Street and Washington Place in Manhattan, New York.

The characters who worked in the factory are fictitious. The incidents which occurred at the factory are a conglomeration of happenings that transpired in numerous sweatshops since their conception. What happened to the Solinskis happened to many families.

Mrs. O.H.P. Belmont, Max Blanck, Isaac Harris, Mary Dreier, Sam Gompers, Clara Lemlich, Magistrate Krotel, Magistrate Breen, Elsie Coke, Elizabeth Dutcher, Violet Pike, Ann Morgan, Mayor McClellan, Miss Marot, John Mitchell, Morris Hillquit, Rabbi Wise, Rose Schneiderman, District Attorney Bostwick, Max D. Steuer and the child Rose, a witness, are real persons.

Works by Penny Hayes

The Long Trail
Yellowthroat
Montana Feathers
Grassy Flats
Kathleen O'Donald

CHAPTER ONE
Wednesday, July 7, 1909

The *Christina Swift* yawed frighteningly as experienced titanic waves tossed the seven-hundred-foot-long steamship like an empty bottle upon the sea. Tons of water sloshed over her decks, drenching the vessel as though the sea had a mind of its own and was only ridding itself of a pesky gnat upon its itching surface. Crew members bellowed curses at the pitiless night and at the ship as they fought to keep her afloat. Thunder aimed its wrath at the hulk; frequent lightning glowed phosphorescent, turning the sky to a metallic light and the surface of the wild sea black as ebony. Aboard the *Christina Swift*, wailing winds filled the hearts of every living soul with terror and dread. The devil himself had cursed them all, and no one was going to get out of this blow alive.

In plush cabins above deck, husbands clung to beds secured to walls; wives and children clung to husbands and fathers. In the hull of the ship immigrants from Germany, Russia, Ireland, England, Scotland, and who knew what other countries, traveled steerage.

In berths stacked one above the other huddled one hundred ninety-eight souls, stranger holding stranger, lover holding lover, families holding families. Bags and sacks hanging from bunks swung sickeningly from side to side, some dislodging and sailing through the air. People frantically grabbed for them, trying to save their meager possessions brought from the Old Country: a precious hand-embroidered handkerchief, a down quilt that invoked warm recollections, a bottle of rye whiskey, a home-cured sausage to preserve the flavor and memory of a former life. The travelers had made hard decisions about which possessions to bring, and to lose them meant to lose one more piece of that past.

The air was thick with the smells of unwashed bodies, urine, old decaying food and seasickness. Filth from poorly ventilated latrines slopped over the seats and onto the floor. Wailing barely recognizable as human was heard above the noise of the storm. Prayers in numerous tongues were fervently voiced.

Above the chaos, children howled in stricken panic as their parents attempted to calm and reassure them.

In a lower bunk, Kathleen Anne O'Donald clutched the side of her bed with one hand while holding a small boy with the other. During one great swell in which the *Christina Swift* rose on a wave to a height of thirty feet only to tear down its lee side, the child had fallen from his mother's arms. Screaming wildly, he grasped at Kathleen as he slid toward her from the berth opposite hers. Momentarily forgetting her own terror, she scooped him up and held him close to her breast. She bent her head near his and sang lullabies in a trembling voice.

Because he was safe in Kathleen's arms, his mother remained where she was, nodding her thanks. With a death grip, she held onto her other three children, all under the ages of seven.

The rolling, pitching motion of the steamship was ceaseless as the boy fought Kathleen, his eyes overflowing with fright. She knew he could not understand English, yet she continued singing to him, feeling as though she were sitting in her own urine. She prayed to God, whom she was certain had deserted them all this night, that it was not true.

Nearby, a blast of lightning struck the ocean's surface. Kathleen shrieked as the almost deafening thunder rolled like a great belch through the ship. The boy in her lap lurched, looked at her and became calm. He laid his head against her breast, closed his eyes and did not move again.

She drew the lad to her, thankful that he had fallen asleep, grateful that he *could* fall asleep, and prayed for all their souls as the storm raged on and on and on.

Over the next four hours the vicious gale pummeled them. By daybreak, and only little by little, did it relinquish its hold upon the *Christina Swift*.

Kathleen glanced down at the sleeping child. About five years old, he was beautiful; long black lashes dripped down his pale cheeks. Black hair fell over his forehead and ears, waving down the back of his neck. His small body felt frail and weightless.

She shifted him against her and spoke to him. He did not respond, and she spoke again. She became alarmed at his inertness as his mother, dragging her other children with her, came to collect him.

Carefully, she took the boy from Kathleen's arms. With a shriek that lifted the hairs on the back of Kathleen's neck, the mother shook the boy, hysterically repeating something in Yiddish. She slapped him sharply, trying to wake him. His eyelids snapped opened, the eyes rolling back until only the whites showed. Shaking and mad with grief, the devastated woman returned to her bed grasping all her children to her, both dead and alive.

Kathleen heard more screams and outcries. Others had perished during the storm. Now freed of the child, she rolled over onto her side, biting into her small canvas bag of belongings so that she, too, would not cry out, would not die, would not give up life.

She ground her teeth, envisioning the funerals likely to occur almost immediately. She doubted there was a choice of taking the bodies to the New World and burying them there. How could they be kept in storage? The trip had been scheduled as a two-week sail. That time had passed, and the rumor was that they were still six days away from America. How, too, could a newcomer to America find and afford a grave, a casket and a man of the cloth right away?

She moaned with the idea of having to make such terrible decisions. Overcome with a crushing sense of grief, she recited an Act of Contrition, hoping the Lord would not care that she had said it swiftly and mechanically. She was certain she was going to die at any moment. She repeated the words with more consideration, while her tears flowed and her jaws ached from gnashing her teeth and biting into the bag.

The pain within her chest subsided as she watched the ship's doctor come down the narrow stairs. His face a wrinkled mask, he held a handkerchief over his nose and mouth as he quickly moved from body to body. He spoke to each relative of the dead, filled out a report, then rapidly departed.

The mother of four, one in her arms, three clutching her heavy black coat, followed him upstairs. Two more bodies, both women, were carried by their husbands. The men grunted their way up the steps, but each handled his burden alone.

Kathleen had occasionally chatted with these families who for days had been traveling with her, who from time to time had shared their hopes and dreams of reaching America after years of religious or political persecution, starvation and certain death at the hands of merciless and relentless rulers or unproductive land.

Now she shared their grief, their losses, the terrible separation of themselves from their greatest gifts. She hoped to God she would never again have to bury someone she loved as she had recently done and as they would do today.

She followed the grievous procession upstairs and onto the deck. Surprisingly, it was a clear and beautiful day. Puffy clouds punched holes in the brilliant blue sky. Already, the sun was caressing the *Christina Swift* with soft colors, brushing her deck dry with warm yellow rays. The ship cut smoothly through a tranquil sea.

Normally, all those below would be on deck by now, breathing the salty refreshing air, letting the wind rake their hair as they gazed westward toward America though it was yet days away. This morning not more than seventy had come up, the others foul with seasickness.

Behind Kathleen came the sounds of a sobbing woman. Two ship's officers carried a large body wrapped in a fine blanket, the weeping woman following closely behind.

In sharp contrast to the thick, drab wool coats, heavy leather shoes and dull brown or black suits and dresses of the immigrants, the woman was clad in a beautiful flowing dress of shimmering black. Silver furs were draped across her slender shoulders. Blond hair piled high on her head remained neatly in place. Her face was carefully made up. She touched her rouged cheekbones as she daintily held a lace handkerchief to the corner of her eye. She looked too beautiful to be genuine. But her grief was real. Kathleen clearly read it in her eyes.

The captain directed the families of the dead and those assisting, to line up along the rail. People respectfully stepped aside as the funeral procession passed by. Officers and seamen stood at attention, ready to give aid and lend to the funeral a semblance of high importance and respect. The lamentations grew louder as the bodies were wrapped in blankets and placed on boards.

The captain's words were brief. Kathleen heard "Amen," and closed her eyes. Flinching inwardly with each sound, she listened to four distinct splashes.

She opened her eyes and observed the mourners. The mother had stopped crying and was now standing without support of friends. She stared at the water's surface for several seconds before going below. The affluent woman, assisted by two officers, staggered back to her stateroom on weakened legs. The widowers knelt side by side, quietly praying. Kathleen, and others who had attended the funerals, backed away, leaving them to grieve alone.

Below deck, Kathleen lay on her bunk and stared at the sagging mattress above her where a sleeping woman loudly snored. At noon, Kathleen was still there as several large pots of lukewarm soup consisting of boiled potatoes and stringy beef were brought below for those who had no food. She did not eat, nor did she choose to eat that evening. She was not sick in body, only in heart.

She lay thinking of Ireland's County Antrim; of its undulating green fields neatly fenced by stone gathered from the meadows. She recalled her mother's satisfied smile each time she pulled from the oven a hot loaf of bread, its delicious odor wafting up and filling the small cottage full of mouth-watering smells. Her father's deep voice echoed in her mind as he repeated a joke he had heard at the pub making them laugh until they thought their sides would split. She refused to think about the overturned cart that had somehow fallen on her mother, instantly killing her, and her father, unable to bear his loss, dying of heart failure not a year later.

She forced herself to think of the exciting find in the wall behind the headboard of her parents' bed. During a thorough cleaning of the cottage, in an attempt to give the place her own identity, she had discovered it. Spotting the crack and exploring further, she found a deliberately loosened chunk of clay. Removing the clay, she revealed a hole that held an iron box full of money. There was not enough to allow her to live leisurely by any means, but it would certainly keep her from starving for the time being.

She thought of the horses, cows and sheep the small farm had supported. She hated taking care of the animals and eventually gave thought to selling them. And then what? That was how the farm made money: by selling wool and milk. She had fended off several offers of marriage. At nineteen, she was not yet ready to make such a commitment. Having been one of her school's brightest scholars, she tried teaching a year and found it dissatisfying. She wanted to do more with her life than raise animals or teach or marry, ending up an old woman with four or five squalling wee ones under foot by the time she reached thirty. She wanted to be happy. She wanted to be rich.

She began to look hard at America.

CHAPTER TWO
Tuesday, July 13, 1909

From her small canvas bag, the same one used when she had bitten back her pain and fear of death, Kathleen pulled out a wooden-handled brush and tiny mirror. Dipping the corner of a small towel she had brought along into her tin cup of water, she wiped away the salt that had collected on her cheeks. Sitting in the corner of her bunk, she tried to pull herself together. She checked her tiny pocket watch. Six A.M. What a day this would be! Today she would see the Statue of Liberty and her very first glimpse of America. She wished to look her best, a task she thought impossible. She studied the sandy-colored lashes that lay against her pallid cheeks and thought that once off this ship her rosy color would reappear, the freckles splashed across her face would once again be prominent, her green eyes flecked with gold, shining. Her forehead was smooth, her neck long. Having lost weight on her five-foot, three-inch frame, she would, in time, fill out again. Her long black hair would glisten again. All she had to do was get off this Goddamn boat! Her hand flew to her mouth. In all her born days she had never cursed. Never! She quickly asked for forgiveness, refusing the tears that fought to surge forth, and smoothed the front of her brown wool dress.

A tall woman passing by paused and, uninvited, sat on the edge of Kathleen's bunk. "Good morning." Her voice was deep, husky, her accent thick as a cockney sailor's. She sat ramrod straight, her graying blond hair braided and encircling her head. Her eyes were a deep slate gray. She was broad-shouldered for a woman, and the dark brown dress she wore accented the sharp angles of her thin body. She was perhaps forty or so. She smiled at Kathleen and asked, "How are you getting on? Well, I hope. I'm from England and —"

"Obviously," Kathleen interrupted. Previously, she had avoided speaking with the woman, knowing she was English, and she bristled at the sound of her broad accent.

"And you're from Ireland."

"That I am," Kathleen answered proudly. The

animosity felt toward the stranger whose monarchy controlled Kathleen's native country, ransacked homes in the night and shot fathers and brothers in Britain's mad obsession to call Ireland England's own soured Kathleen's mouth with venom. "And I'll thank you to get off my bed."

The smile faded from the woman's face, shock and dejection filling her eyes. The color in her cheeks changed from the pallid look prevalent amongst those who had for twenty-one days lived in this hole to a red reserved only for the sick. She seemed to shrink before Kathleen's eyes.

The woman stood, backed off a little, and looked at her.

"You're angry at me. I understand why, and I'm sorry. I apologize for bothering you."

Kathleen scowled at her receding back, then began to brush her hair, tearing at it vengefully, angry that this Englishwoman would presume to sit upon her bed without first asking. Her fingers flew as she braided her tress into a thick plait to hang freely down her back.

A loud shout came from above. "America! I can see America!"

People bounded off bunks and scrambled to be first up the stairs. Swept along with the joyful immigrants, Kathleen saw that others, already five deep, lined the railing of the deck. Men held their children high above their heads so that they could see the great Statue of Liberty reaching over three hundred feet into the air, the statue still only a hazy outline against the horizon. On the mainland, buildings stretched to the sky, creating a second obscure backdrop. Children darted between feet, making their way to the railing. Adults struggled to move away from the crush behind them while others fought to take their places. Exhilarated cries in multiple languages rang in the air. Tears of both joy and fear ran freely. The excitement was nearly tangible. A single thought passed through Kathleen's mind: she had achieved her dream; she had made it all the way across the ocean to America.

On deck above steerage, first- and second-class travelers pointed at the great monument. Excitedly chatting and laughing, the women wore light dresses, the men lightweight suits.

Kathleen spotted the affluent woman whose husband had died six days ago. Blankly staring toward shore, she wore the same black dress as she had the day of the funerals. She was still beautiful, but her face seemed devoid of life. Again, Kathleen felt a stirring empathy toward her. The death of a loved one, she thought, equally affected everyone.

Her chest constricted as she thought of how alone she would be without friends or family in this strange new land. Everybody in her hamlet of Glarryford had told her outright she had lost her sanity. They swore the Little People had bewitched her. When advised by neighbors to talk to Father O'Dey, their priest, she did and also to a few well-meaning friends who had known her since birth. It had not quieted them, but discussing her plans with them had only made her more determined to leave. There was more to life than what northern Ireland's County Antrim could offer.

The crowd thinned somewhat, and at last she reached the rail. She could see the statue now, the Lady's torch uplifted, her gown flowing and graceful, her arm clutched around the Truth of America, and in her shadow, the red-brick buildings of Ellis Island.

The ship steamed through the Narrows of New York Harbor. Kathleen remained where she was, staring with nearly unblinking eyes first at the Goddess of Liberty and then at the island itself. Gazing at the statue, she felt the first trembling of love and an almost sexual urge while studying the figure's mouth.

The acrolith was huge now. The ship was as close to it as it would come, the monument towering above the newcomers, inviting them, welcoming them. Unable to reach it, Kathleen still stretched her hand toward the Lady.

"We've come to a new land. We've come to start over. Let the men do what they think they must do. Let you and me begin again."

The Englishwoman stood beside Kathleen.

"You! Why do you bother me?"

"I don't understand German, Italian, Yiddish, Russian and whatever else is being spoken on this boat," the woman replied in her husky cockney voice. She, too, wore the headscarf, the dark coat, the practical heavy shoes that the rest of the immigrants wore. "I have little interest in talking to English families. I find they are completely absorbed in their own lives."

"I believe you," Kathleen admitted, instantly regretting having given anything of herself to the stranger.

The woman placed strongly veined hands on the rail. "We're alone, you and me, and I offer you me company and plead for yours in return. Each of us can get through Ellis Island much easier if a friend stands beside us. Especially since we travel without husbands."

Kathleen's anger flared. "I don't need a friend, and I certainly don't need a husband. I'm quite capable doing for myself."

The woman pulled back in surprise. "Not even need a friend today? Everyone needs someone today. Everyone! Here, even God Himself needs a friend." Her voice became impassioned. "It'll be a hard day today, lass. A father, a wife, yes, and maybe even a child will not be allowed to stay. Families will make the choice of a lifetime — whether to stay as a family or to separate, some to stay, some to go. Some will go directly to jail. Some will die of heartbreak and homesickness before they travel fifty miles to their next destination. And to be unmarried is to tempt the authorities to refuse you entry to the United States. That is, unless you have a man who will vouch for your employment."

"What makes you such an expert, English-woman?"

"Her husband." She turned and looked at the deck above them. Kathleen followed her gaze to the ship's recent widow. "You know her?"

"I was Mr. and Mrs.'s servant when they visited England. He spoke at length to me about America. I asked him about coming here. He told me wonderful things about the United States."

"The wealthy don't speak to servants except to order them about," Kathleen said. "Even I know that much about them."

"He did. He wasn't quite as bad as the rest. He spoke to us all. There were several of us who worked for Mr. and Mrs. They both asked me if I would come to America and serve them. I agreed."

"But you travel steerage."

"I'm a servant, not a rich woman. I helped them on ship during the days. Since his death, I've been dismissed effective when we land. The Mrs. can't stand seeing anyone that reminds her of him. I apparently do."

"Then you've been stranded."

"Not exactly. I've been given a letter for other servant's employment." The woman patted her bosom to indicate the letter's location. "The Mrs. is allowing me to stay in her servants' quarters only until that time. She doesn't even want me traveling with her to her home today. I'm to make my own way there. Otherwise, being an unmarried lady, I'd have to return to England. She's told the ship's captain that I may leave Ellis Island. It's been entered in the ship's manifest."

Fear clutched at Kathleen's throat. Unseeing, she watched the dark water sliding by. The air was sucked from her lungs, her throat closing. She must go to the United States. She must!

"I have no husband. I didn't know," she uttered. Urgently and desperately she searched her mind for a quick solution. The island was swiftly approaching. In moments they would arrive. The authorities mustn't send her back. She shuddered at the thought of a return voyage. The dreams she had harbored since her decision to come here, the prayers she had said, all the candles she had lighted loomed in her mind. She could not go back!

Possibly the Englishwoman could help her. But the woman was *English.* An enemy! Yet, there was no other way. She forced herself to look directly at her adversary. Swallowing her zealous pride, Kathleen said, "I will pay you whatever you wish if you will ask your lady to write me a letter of reference. I'm a schoolteacher and a good Catholic. I . . ." She fought the desire to strangle the fool who made up such a cruel dictate that a woman needed a husband to enter this country. At the age of twenty, why wasn't a woman old enough to be able to lead her own life without having to lean on a man for her every breath?

She felt like chattel.

"I'll be back." Just like that, the woman left. She returned within a half hour. "Here's your letter." She held out a sealed envelope. Her hand shook violently. Her eyes were deeply pained. "The Mrs. can be very difficult at times. She'll be glad to be rid of me, and I, of her."

Her own hands trembling and feeling traitorous to her motherland, Kathleen accepted the indispensable letter.

The woman's kindness mystified her. It was a great favor — that much was obvious — and the woman had had to fight to get the letter. She dreaded the amount the woman would demand. Kathleen would give up all of her money except for twenty-five dollars. An immigrant had to have twenty-five dollars. How had she learned about this silly rule and not the one concerning husbands? No matter! She had the reference in her hands; right now it was worth any price.

"How much do I owe you?" she asked.

"Nothing. You need help. I need help. It's payment enough."

Kathleen studied her nemesis, contemplating their mutual ancient, and recent, history. She felt her veins fill with an inexplicable conflagration. Her throat burned as though she had just vomited. She swallowed the threatening bile. The Englishwoman had been generous beyond reason. Kathleen battled to keep that before her.

The steamship's horn let out a long, powerful blast. En masse the passengers jumped. Babies screamed. As a group, they laughed at one another. Kathleen's tension seemed to melt away, and she laughed too.

She leaned against the rail, staring at Ellis Island, now a massive edifice with an American flag positioned before it. The banner fluttered strongly in the breeze at the top of a tall pole. "I thank you deeply," she said. "While we're being processed, I'll stay with you. I won't call you friend, nor do I want to have anything to do with you after we reach New York City. I'm aware of how much I owe you. But I cannot forget what you English have done to us."

"Thank you," the woman replied with a trace of acridity.

Kathleen refused to be embarrassed.

"Me name," she told Kathleen, "is Rose Stewart."

"I am Kathleen Anne Mary O'Donald," Kathleen returned rigidly.

Rose Stewart looked toward the island. From the corner of her eye, Kathleen examined her. Tiny crow's feet stretched out from Rose's eyes. Her brows were thick and black, her eyes a slate gray. Her lips were thin but seemed to hold strength. She had yet to be missing any teeth; they were strong-looking and straight as a child's. But for the heavy tea stains they would have been perfect. Rose Stewart was not too unattractive for an Englishwoman.

The ship slowed and docked at Pier 43, one of many Hudson River piers that lined lower Manhattan. "They're going to let first-class and cabin-class passengers off here," Rose said.

"Not us?" Kathleen watched the fortunate ones stroll down the gangplank and onto their newly adopted homeland. "We don't leave?"

"Not bloody likely," Rose answered. "They were processed on board yesterday." On the upper deck, boys carried heavy bags and baggage. Porters wheeled large dressing lockers on dollies down the plank. "We're going to be taken back to Ellis Island. It's there we get processed."

"What's the difference between them and me?" Kathleen asked.

"Money, a good job, sometimes a bribe."

"It's unfair."

"Aye, it is, Kathleen O'Donald, but that's life, and you'd best be getting used to it in this America."

After the favored ones had disembarked, the immigrants left the ship to board the ferry for the fifteen-minute trip to the island. Loaded and packed body to body, many from other docked ships, they traveled on the upper deck opened to the elements while baggage was stored on the lower deck.

Kathleen and Rose made sure they stood by the rail. The clean, crisp wind bathing their faces, Kathleen again marveled at the Statue. The sensuous sensation returned as she studied each feature of the Lady. She swallowed and breathed deeply of American air and mentally blew a kiss to the Goddess.

Upon docking, the barge unloaded immediately, Kathleen and Rose staying carefully beside each other as the crowd disembarked. Their ferry having docked along with several others, the women could easily have become separated by hundreds of anxious people lining up four abreast for entrance to the processing center. English or not, Kathleen found herself grateful for Rose's presence and felt a whit less frightened with her there.

As they left the gangplank, almost to a person, everyone bore something: a small satchel, a large basket, a cloth sack slung over a shoulder, a child or two or three. Kathleen carried her precious canvas bag; Rose, a single small, worn leather suitcase. They were given a dark piece of bread and a cup of coffee or a glass of milk by men and women waiting on the docks and whose job it was to be sure every immigrant received something to eat.

Rose passed her bread and milk to a child in front of her. The little boy looked grateful. Kathleen witnessed for a second time this morning Rose's spontaneous generosity.

The new arrivals were directed to the main building and into the Great Hall. Kathleen shrank beneath its massive size: over two hundred feet long, one hundred feet wide and fifty-six feet to the ceiling.

"Why, it seems you could put my entire hamlet in here," she whispered.

"And mine," Rose whispered back.

They were herded through a maze of passageways with iron-pipe railings. People of all ages were laughing — or crying, talking incessantly —

or keeping silent. Some seemed to be enjoying the entire experience, others not at all. All clearly wore their feelings upon their faces and in their eyes. A friend or family member became an island of safety, Kathleen thought, where it appeared that nothing but a familiar hand or arm could give comforting shelter.

"Yer in the pens now," she heard a man tell a boy beside him, and indeed, she was reminded of the cattle pens she had seen near Glarryford.

As she shuffled along someone pinned a number to her chest. It seemed days before she reached the first team of doctors, one of whom put her through a brief medical examination. Several people before her had been singled out, a prominent chalk mark drawn down the backs of their shirts or coats. Marked for a more intensive examination, Kathleen observed stark terror flood their eyes as they were led away from the general flow of traffic.

Two hours later she and Rose reached the final team of doctors at the front of the line. Although benches lined the pens, Kathleen's feet and back ached from continuous standing. She had yielded her seat yet again to the mother with four small children following behind.

Using a button hook, a doctor quickly flipped her eyelids inside out. The pain was unexpected and frightening. She thought she would faint. As he worked, he asked her to cough and studied her face, hair, neck and hands.

In the pen to her left, an interpreter was speaking for a Russian man and his family and answering questions for the doctor. They began to converse rapidly. The father fell to his knees before the examiner as the mother began sobbing loudly. She clutched two wide-eyed children to her bosom.

"He's going back home," Kathleen overheard the doctor say. "He has trachoma. Five minutes ago one came through with tuberculosis. Don't know how they missed it at the first inspection."

"Move him out," came the cold order.

Kathleen watched the man stagger to a bench, one of many at the ends of the cages and filled with tear-streaked faces. His wife held his arm; his children grasped their mother's coat. All this way, Kathleen thought, all the dreams — gone, the hopes — gone, the prayers useless.

Her heart began to thunder and rage. She had never doubted that she would be allowed to enter America, to become a citizen of this great country. Now she did. She had just seen it happen as Rose had said it might. She felt light-headed and reached back to touch Rose, to have the Englishwoman's nearness steady her.

Rose took her hand and squeezed it. Kathleen averted her eyes from the Russian family, the husband with his head between his knees, his wife with her hands full, holding their children and trying to comfort her husband.

"Move ahead," the impatient doctor said to Kathleen.

Those who made it past the doctors were then herded before uniformed immigration inspectors. On their desks before them were various ships' manifests listing basic information regarding each passenger and filled out by the ships' officers at the port of origin.

Kathleen's inspector's great bushy eyebrows came together in a fierce scowl as he fired question after question at her. "Who paid your ship's fare? Where are you going? Can you read and write? Have you ever been in prison? Do you have at least twenty-five dollars? Show it to me. Where did you get it?"

He inquired about her marital status, skills, and personal history. She gave her age and said no, she had no job but she expected to be working in a factory in less than a week. She had already decided to take any factory job offered her. "No," she answered his next abrupt question, she had no relatives here.

Over her shoulder, Rose quickly said, "But I'm her cousin, and we've come here together."

Kathleen lowered her eyes. She hated a liar, but she instinctively knew that this was a necessary lie. A woman alone was in constant danger, and she had not prepared for this at all. She asked the Lord to forgive her and responded, "Sure, that's true. We joined up in England, and Rose already has a job." Now she had cursed. Now she had lied. Was this the land of sin as well as of new life?

Eventually the questions stopped, and with fingers trembling, she clutched the hoped-for landing card handed her, admitting her to the United States of America.

She waited off to one side while Rose crisply and confidently answered the brisk inspector. Then Rose, too, gripping the precious card, passed through the pen and into her new country.

Rose took her arm. "They're going to feed us before we leave. We can get something to eat this way. I can smell the food cooking, and we'd better stop at the money exchange on the way."

Kathleen felt as if she were being pulled along by Rose even though Rose had now let go of her arm. It had not been an uncomfortable feeling at all to let someone else take charge for at least a few minutes.

They were given box lunches of ham sandwiches, a banana and weak, sugarless coffee. On a bench in a large dining hall filled with hundreds of other immigrants, they devoured the food and drink in a few short minutes. They were handed a second box to take with them aboard the ferry and then the train for the ride to their next destination.

"Well," Kathleen said, abstractedly brushing crumbs from her lap. "I guess this is goodbye. They'll be calling us for the ferry to New York City soon."

Rose frowned. "You have no bloody idea where you're going, do you?"

"Vaguely," Kathleen bravely answered. "And I've heard that New York City is a place to get rich. The Lord will provide. He has so far."

"You better hope He'll provide for you, Kathleen Anne Mary O'Donald." Rose pulled her suitcase closer to her feet. "Because He's got millions of souls He's watching out for, and that keeps Him busy. I just hope he has time for you, lassie."

24

CHAPTER THREE

Tuesday, July 13, 1909

Kathleen and Rose huddled together with the hundreds of others already through the pens as they prepared to board the ferry and then trains that would take them into the heart of New York City, to New Jersey and to points south and west.

"My letter of recommendation is for a residence in New York City," Rose said. "I'm to be a house servant there, if they take me. It looks like we're to ride the same train."

Kathleen reacted with concealed relief. "I guess that'd be all right."

"Do you really intend to work in a factory?" Rose asked. They moved forward a foot or so as the line slowly inched its way toward the ticket window.

"At the very first one that'll hire me," Kathleen answered. "A clothing one probably. It's about all I expect I'll be qualified to do — sew." She shifted her belongings from one hand to the other. "I need to start right away and to find a place to stay." She looked at her watch. "One o'clock. There's still time." Weariness permeated her bones. She had been on the go without letup since six this morning.

Rose shook her head in dismay. "You have more nerve than brains, child."

Kathleen glared at Rose. "I've come clear across the ocean alone and have done just fine. A child alone couldn't have done that."

Rose's lips drew into a tight smile. "No doubt you'd have come through customs in fine fiddle, too."

Kathleen pulled back her shoulders and lifted her chin. "That's right. And I'll be reminding you that you were the one who asked for help."

"What makes you so stubborn?"

"You presume to know me. Don't."

Bolts of anger darted into Rose's eyes. "My, you're a feisty one."

"I'm Irish. You're English."

"I'm an American now, and so are you. We've left our countries. We're two women alone. We should stop arguing and help each other. Not continue this stupid fight."

"I didn't start it."

Rose stepped out of line. "And neither did I." Her eyes filled with confusion and pain. "I was born into the fray just as you were. I'm glad to be shed of it, and I have no intentions of carrying me country's burdens to this new land. Apparently you do. Goodbye, Kathleen Anne Mary O'Donald. I wish you well in your new life." She turned abruptly and with stiff, brittle dignity, walked to the end of the long line.

A harrowing headache began to pound against the inside of Kathleen's forehead. Another country. Yes, she was in another country. New battles to be fought. How could it be otherwise? There was always a battle of some kind going on somewhere.

She had behaved shamefully, pouncing so severely upon Rose who wanted only companionship through Ellis Island, and she had done nothing but wage war with her. She studied the floor, swallowed her pride and joined the Englishwoman.

Deliberately, Rose turned her back as Kathleen approached.

Kathleen drew in a deep breath, then slowly released it. "I apologize, Rose Stewart. It's been a long and bitter feud between us."

Rose's back stiffened. Her voice was cold, stubborn. "It hasn't been between us. I've never seen you before twenty-four, June. It hasn't been between us, I say. Calling you a child still makes sense to me."

Kathleen's hostility reared again. "I don't like . . ." Her words died upon her lips. She had said enough. She moved to stand beside Rose. "It'll take another hour to get back to where we started."

Rose looked at her, her eyes softening. Cryptically, she said, "No, I don't think so. I think this is where we start."

"Sure, you're right, Rose Stewart."

At last they reached the windows. Overcome with exhaustion, Kathleen wanted only to lie down on one of the benches and sleep. Instead, she boarded the Ellis Island ferry which would take her to the Manhattan piers. From there, she would take a train and then the El down Sixth Avenue to that section of the city where most of the factories were located, according to Father O'Dey who had once studied in New York City.

On the ferry, she ate her box lunch, then pulled from her sack a small notebook in which were carefully penciled several possibilities given to her by O'Dey. At the top of the list was written: *Triangle Shirtwaist Company, Asch Building, Washington Place and Greene Street.* She would try there first.

The *Ellis Island* docked at Manhattan. As nervous as she was, she stepped with great pride from the ferry onto American soil. People greeted others as they came ashore. There were gleeful shouts as relative found relative and friend found friend. Laughter and tears flowed freely as distant travelers flung themselves into the warmth and security of waiting arms.

On Ellis Island, several women had married not three hours previously; some women had prearranged their marriages before leaving their home country. Arriving without jobs, their new husbands provided them with the other essential ingredient needed before being allowed to board the ferry for the mainland — a male relative. From a distance and outdoors through an opened window, Kathleen had briefly watched one such marriage take place while clutching Rose's letter in her pocket. The wedding had seemed so fraudulent.

Single men and men in groups not expecting anyone, immediately began walking toward the city into the unknown. Kathleen watched several of them go facing a future Kathleen was sure would lay before them streets paved with gold and riches beyond belief, a vision that could not be matched or challenged anywhere else on earth.

In no time it seemed, some of those with whom Kathleen had lived the better part of three weeks in intimate quarters disappeared into electric streetcars, automobiles, trains and horse carriages. She would never see those people again, she thought as she waved goodbye to several who had bunked nearby. She felt their departure as strongly as one might anticipate a long separation from a beloved family member.

"I've never seen anything like it," Rose said. Her face paled as she watched the group disperse. She stood so close that Kathleen could feel Rose's arm touching her own. "I always thought nothing could bother me."

Aboard her train, her bag tucked securely beside her, Kathleen looked around, feeling as though New York was about to devour her. Dozens of rails headed away from the piers and into the city, the transport trains often yielding to the more luxurious passenger trains. She watched her vista change from open ocean and the beautiful Statue to towering buildings shutting out much of the sun's light. She was now part of the city, part of the rush. She had, she believed, become part of the buildings themselves.

The train stopped, the immigrants reaching a large station where several trolley cars waited.

"Which one?" Kathleen asked the equally frightened Rose. "Which one?"

The street was lined with the tallest structures Kathleen had ever seen. Eight, nine and ten stories high, the buildings began closing in on her and remembering her observations from the *Christina Swift,* she knew these were just the smaller buildings. Miles of wire were strung across the streets connecting pole to building and building to building. As she walked beside Rose, she had an irrational moment of fear at the thought of the wires falling down on her and electrocuting her on the spot. She was struck with a second illogical fear that these structures made of brick and wood might crumble and collapse, burying her beneath a great heap of rubble.

Rose had pulled her letter from a breast pocket and was closely studying it. "It looks like I'll be taking a trolley in this direction. The Mrs. was good enough to draw me a map." Her finger trailed a small sketch toward lower Fifth Avenue.

"Did she happen to mention where Greene and Washington streets are?" Kathleen was about to be left alone. Now — right now! There would be no Rose, no one to fight with, no one but complete strangers to help her with directions. Proper ladies did not talk to strangers.

"No, but we'll ask," Rose boldly said. Nearby, several uniformed men were directing the new arrivals to their trolley cars and various destinations.

A bewhiskered officer explained briefly how the two women were to reach theirs. "You should both take the El on Sixth. It'll get you closer faster." Focusing his attention on Kathleen, he offered her an address where she might take a room on Wooster Street between Houston and Bleecker. "They're always looking for boarders of quality. I'm sure they'll be pleased to see you." Looking rather satisfied with himself, he handed her a slip of paper containing the address.

As the two women moved away, Rose said, "I don't trust the looks of him. I bet he gets a payback if you take the room."

"We'll ask another," Kathleen said.

They did and heard the directions repeated, including that of the boardinghouse. Rose picked up her suitcase. "I don't trust either one of them, now. Me father used to have a job like that, directing people from the trains going into London. He got paid for every head he placed."

"Were they bad places?" Kathleen asked, only half listening.

"Sometimes. Depended on how the poor bloke was dressed. Here. Let's get on the El."

They had walked a block and a half to reach it and now climbed aboard. It was now nearing three o'clock. Kathleen hoped she did not have much farther to go. She abhorred the idea of riding a train in the air, but finding lodging and a job today outweighed the distaste and fear of the El.

She gawked at the tall buildings as they rode south into the blinding sun. She could not imagine what held them up. A big barn had always been a wonder to her, and here was construction reaching to the sky. It sickened her to think of being so high in the air. She looked down at the street below her as the El rounded a slight curve and prayed that the factory would allow her to remain on the first floor. But then there was the troublesome thought of all that weight from wood and machinery and stone balanced above her.

She fought vertigo, looking at her feet until the nausea passed. Rose must have been watching her. Strong fingers pressed reassuringly on her arm. Kathleen smiled weakly and turned her eyes again to the floor.

"How can you stand this?" she asked.

"I'm not doing so well, but I was raised in London, and that helps. There are sights like this all over the city. They're a wonder, ain't they?"

"They're frightening, that's what they are. I'll never get used to them"

Rose shifted in her seat as the El swayed to and fro. "Why did you leave Ireland, Kathleen? I understand your country is spacious and green and beautiful."

"It is." Kathleen again gaped at her surroundings and listened to the dreadful noise of the El. "But I hope to become rich here."

"And do what with your money?"

"That I hadn't decided except to make enough to not have to take care of animals or to get married quite so young or teach. I didn't like that, either. I heard America was the place to come and make money."

Rose's serious look disturbed Kathleen. "We'll see, won't we, the both of us?"

Kathleen nodded. "But where are all the beautiful places in America?"

"I'm sure I don't know."

The El made numerous stops along Sixth Avenue, and now it was Kathleen's turn to get off. She was tired beyond belief. Perhaps it would be smarter if she just rested today and applied for a position tomorrow when she felt better. She could certainly use not moving around for a few hours.

"It looks like you should walk from here," Rose said, as the El pulled to a halt at Fourteenth Street. "Good luck, Kathleen."

Her stomach queasy, Kathleen rose from her seat. "Good luck to you as well, Rose Stewart. Come and visit me when you're a fine lady riding in a fine carriage."

"Likely I won't be coming here," Rose answered, looking around at the dismal surroundings.

Kathleen stepped into the street. For the first time today, she dared to, had to remove her coat, though not her hat. The heat was unbearable. She stubbed her toe on a chunk of cobblestone as she stepped onto the sidewalk. The El was already gone and with it, Rose.

She was at the corner of Sixth and Fourteenth. According to her directions, she was to head south until she found Bleecker. Before she hit Houston, she should have found the address the man had handed her back at the trolley station. Not knowing where else to look for immediate rooming, she decided to take his advice.

Brazenly, she asked for clarification of directions at the end of each block. Some people were very kind to her, others rude and the worst, those who asked her to . . . to . . . She forced her thoughts away from those men, concentrating only on achieving her destination. Instinctively, she knew she had walked too far when she hit Broome Street. More directions from more strangers put her on Wooster now heading north.

She passed canyons of rowhouses. The dismal decaying brownstones lining each side of Wooster seemed identical. The floors of the alleys between the buildings looked like repositories of all the rubbish from the past decade. Between various buildings were strung a myriad of ropes on pulleys. From the ropes hung limp laundry of dingy and worn clothing. There were opened metal stairways attached to the outside of the buildings. They led to small landings protected by railings, stopping at each floor. The railings were also draped with wet clothing.

People were out on them now sitting in the shady part of the building. Some women sat with babes in their arms. Several old men slept on the landings. Kathleen thought the stairs were a way to escape the edifices if fires should occur. It was the first good idea she had noted about the city since she had exited the El.

On the sidewalks, energetic children of varying ages shouted and romped together playing ball and hopscotch and jumping rope. They seemed to belong to no one and simply ran merrily about. Old women and men sat on steps chatting in the afternoon sun. From opened windows above, others called down to them or across the street to neighbors. Shopkeepers lazily lounged against opened doorways, some proprietors clad only in pants, shoes and brief undershirts. Kathleen averted her eyes as they whistled at her or encouraged her to shop.

Baking heat seeped through the soles of her shoes and radiated from the buildings. Sweat dripped from her face and from the faces of all who lived within Wooster's confines.

Driven more by panic than the necessity to reach Wooster as quickly as possible, she was there in thirty minutes. She again glanced at the address in her hand and at the apartment building looming before her. It was fully five stories high, the entrance a double door. Above that and to either side, were tall windows, four across. A *For Rent* sign was propped in the lower right window.

Bravely, she stepped past two seated men talking together on the steps. "Pardon me," she said politely. They shifted as she made her way past them. Inside, the place smelled of cat urine and human excrement. Odors of rancid grease and garlic hung heavily in the air. Wallpaper peeled from water-stained walls. The railing to the steps leading to the floors above was partially missing. The floor was worn clean of any paint that may have once existed upon its surface.

"Good heavens," Kathleen whispered. "I've entered the devil's own dwelling." Surely, she had been misdirected by the men at the station.

She started to leave when to her left, a door opened. The largest woman Kathleen had ever seen stepped out. "You here for a room?" the woman thundered. "Who sent ya? I have some of the boys down the station keeping a sharp eye out for single women. They're the ones needs the most and fastest help. What's yer name?"

"Kathleen O'Donald, I . . ." She backed away as the woman shuffled toward her on battered slippers; tight curly hair dyed a bright red was mounded in a great globe about her head. A dress the size of a small tent covered her massive body. Piercing blue eyes, a tiny nose and rosebud lips peeked out of corpulent folds that made up her face. Standing a head and a half taller than Kathleen, the woman terrified her.

As if sensing her fear, the stranger said, "Relax, honey. I'm not dangerous, just mighty big." She smiled, her face lighting up. "Name's Grace. Ain't that a killer? The only time I'm graceful is in twenty feet of water, and that don't happen too often around here." She laughed uproariously, slapping her huge belly with broad hands. "Come on, girlie, I'll show you yer room. You'll be sharing an apartment. Big, though. Bathroom's down the hall from it."

She grabbed Kathleen firmly by the elbow, propelling her toward stairs running up through the center of the building. Puffing her way up three flights, she stopped at a door devoid of paint and gustily yelled, "Hey, Benjamin, I got a live one. She'll do good. For a while at least," she added in a much softer voice. "You young girls that come from England —"

"Ireland," Kathleen quickly corrected.

Frowning, Grace repeated, "Ireland, then. And Russia and Poland and God knows where else. Don't you have better ways there than here?"

Kathleen finally managed to free her arm. "We don't think so. That's why we come to America."

Grace laughed so hard her face turned beet red. She slapped her belly again. Kathleen feared the big woman would die of heart failure right before her eyes.

Grace banged on the door. "Come on, Benjamin. I know you're in there. You can take a minute to answer the Goddamn door."

A man drenched in sweat from his head to his trousers belt, opened the door. His suspenders hung along his pants legs and a long-sleeved, soaked white shirt adhered like skin to his body. His face looked worn even behind his bushy beard. Behind him, Kathleen could see a woman and child laboring at a table.

"Working hard?" Grace said to Benjamin. She tee-heed, looking at Kathleen as if she had shared a great joke.

"Always," came his tired reply. "Glad to see you, miss," he said politely, with an accent Kathleen could barely understand.

"Come on in, Kathleen. This here's Benjamin Solinski. We'll dig you out a corner to sleep in." Benjamin went back to work as Grace pushed Kathleen through the door. "That'll be five dollars a month," Grace said.

Kathleen blanched at her surroundings as she followed Grace inside. The apartment could not have been more than twelve feet wide. They had entered a long kitchen. A couple of rooms to her right led her to believe they might be bedrooms, but she couldn't be sure. Walls were bare of any kind of decorations or pictures; in spots, faded wallpaper was peeling away. The apartment was lighted from the outside by windows opened to allow in what breeze might be available. Buzzing flies were madly zooming in and out and around the cramped quarters. On a large kitchen table heaped high with wool coat pieces and hosting a couple of straight-back chairs was centered a kerosene lantern, the only implement Kathleen saw that would light this place later. There was a treadle sewing machine which Benjamin was already busily operating, a two-burner gas stove and a double bed buried beneath more work yet to come. A porcelain sink overflowed with unfinished clothing. Pieces of trousers, shirtwaists and cloaks were stacked high against the walls, beneath the table, and extending into the rooms Kathleen noticed earlier. There was not one iota of space in which one might freely move about or truly relax.

Rudely pointing to each person working at the table, Grace said, "This here's Sadie, Benjamin's wife, and his daughter, Sasha." Sadie was a small thin woman in her late twenties who appeared tense and cautious. Her long, bony face was made of deep, shadowy angles, and her large brown eyes were fierce with determination. Sasha was approximately nine years old and a duplicate of her mother with the exception of those big, dark eyes still filled with youthful hope.

Sadie and Sasha's brown dresses were worn thin. They busily shook off annoying flies landing on their sweating faces and arms as they hand-stitched coat pieces of varying designs, rich in fabric, color and texture. The heavy wool draped across the table and over their laps wrapped them, Kathleen imagined, in soaring temperatures. They quickly greeted Kathleen, barely pausing in their work.

Kathleen was given a quick tour of the other two rooms which were filled with more work to do. Dazed, she failed to see where the girl slept. Only the double bed was visible. She impatiently brushed away a fly that persisted in landing on her cheek.

"I really don't know if I want to stay here," she said to Grace. She had not yet spotted what would be her own sleeping area.

Grace seemed to read her mind. "You can look at other boardinghouses, dearie, but I run the cleanest. Nice air shafts, plenty of light." Kathleen didn't think so. "Hang your laundry in the shaft if you've a mind to. You ain't supposed to but people do anyway. We got hot water here, too."

A dark cloud settled over Kathleen as she glanced from the door to the confining room and back to the door again. There was no place here for her to rest while everyone else was laboring so hard.

In one corner of the room, Grace shoved aside a stack of fabric, revealing several empty soapboxes. Three thick boards rested across them. With flair, Grace said, "Yer bed. Sleep in or on your coat or this cloth here, and you'll be comfortable. Right, Benjamin?" she called over her shoulder to the man hunched over the machine, furiously sewing a piece of lining to a sleeve.

Sluggishly, Kathleen set her bag on the crude bed, unable to bear the thought of looking for another place today. Somehow, she would get through this night and then move on tomorrow.

"I'm telling ya, Kathleen, dear, if yer thinking of

39

looking today for someplace else to rent, you'll find the same affair everywhere. Yer in factory territory now. Better get used to it. I'll take the money now. You gonna work for Benjamin here?" she asked, expectantly holding out her hand for the rent. "You can do contract work for other dotes and never leave your happy home."

Kathleen doubted this place ever saw a happy moment. "I plan to look for factory work first," she answered. She had no idea people could stay home and work.

"Then give me the fiver now, and you can go factory hunting. My guess is you'll be working before the day's done."

As the dull ache of reality set in, Kathleen turned away from Grace and fished around in her coat pocket for five precious one-dollar bills.

Grace counted them and gave one to Benjamin. "Here ya are, Benjamin. Meat on the table tonight." Benjamin snatched the bill from her hand and rammed it into his pocket. He was sewing again almost without having missed a stitch.

"Where you gonna look first?" Grace asked. "Maybe I can help ya."

Kathleen did not want to tell Grace, but what would have been the point of keeping it from her? "A place called Triangle Shirtwaist Company on Greene Street and Washington Place."

"I know it. Good place to work. You'll get a job there, for sure. For that matter, anyplace you try, you'll get work. But lucky for you, the Triangle's only a few blocks from here. Big park near there. Washington Square. Go north up Wooster. You'll run right into it in no time. Come on," Grace said at the door. "I'll walk you downstairs. The lass'll be home from work about eight, Benjamin. Let her in. Don't forget now."

Boxes! She would be sleeping on soapboxes tonight. Kathleen refused to cry.

Carrying her coat with her, she followed Grace who descended the stairs in a lilting fashion that reminded Kathleen of the sailors she had often watched walking across the rolling decks of the *Christina Swift*.

At Grace's door, Kathleen asked, "Isn't eight a little late for coming home from work?"

"Actually, it's early. It could be ten or even eleven and you ain't done and having to bring yer work home to finish. See you later, maybe. Triangle starts on the eighth floor. Good luck." She reached her door and was gone as it closed with a bang.

Kathleen stood in dumb silence. The Triangle *started* on the eighth floor? She remained immobilized at the very idea of working in the sky until a child of about ten burst through the door and scampered by her. His high-pitched voice woke her from her awful daydream.

"Outta the way, lady!"

"Hello," she managed to croak. She made herself walk through the door he had left open, and down the stairs. She turned up Wooster Street and on unsteady feet, headed toward Greene and Washington.

CHAPTER FOUR
Tuesday, July 13, 1909

Kathleen reached Washington Square Park in less than fifteen minutes. Even though noisy trolleys traveled around the park, she found the park itself exhilarating to look upon with its wonderful greenery in such sharp contrast to the cars and surrounding buildings. A uniformed patrolman proudly astride his horse on one of the bridle paths, passed close by tipping his hat. Shrill shouts of children at play on the grass or splashing around within a large circular fountain centered in the turf, filled the hot summer afternoon. Numerous people sat beneath shady trees. Brownstone, red brick and limestone homes surrounded the greensward. One larger brick building housed New York University. A stunning church on the southwest corner of the park attracted her. She wandered over to read its name: Judson Memorial Church. She would have to find the Catholic church as soon as possible.

At the base of Fifth Avenue guarding the northern entrance to the park was a great fifty-foot-high arch supported by two enormous pillars. Kathleen approached it and placed a solemn hand upon its warm surface. The edifice looked to be made of granite. Marveling at the structure, she estimated each post at least eight feet thick and ten feet wide. She imagined she could drive three or four milk wagons side by side beneath the arch and never touch either column.

Backing away, she glanced upward. On each pillar was carved a duplicate coat of arms and swords where the arch began its amazing curve. Two angels wrapped themselves along the bend of the arch. A large bird, an eagle perhaps, was centered above the arch itself with a row of flowery wreaths extending off either side. The structure's wide underside was embellished with five rows of wreaths, each encased in a small neat box and extending from one side of the curve to the other. Kathleen again touched the arch with reverence and at the same time, violent confusion that such a wonderful design was conceived and created by man, just as was her abhorrent apartment.

She left the park and walked east on Waverly

Place to the corner of Greene Street and turned south following sidewalks eight feet wide. The street sliced a narrow path between towering buildings. Horse-drawn wagons loaded with crates and boxes of vegetables occupied the curbs. The street was lined with busy shops, office buildings and factories, smoke belching out of their lofty stacks. To Kathleen's eyes, each structure seemed a duplicate of its neighbor — tall, brick or granite with dozens of large windows stacked like dominos end to end that ran from ground to roof. Rails with rumbling trolleys ran down the middle of the cobbled boulevard. Busy people hustled by, untalking, heads bent, determined looks on set faces. Suit coats were draped over men's arms with hats pushed back on damp foreheads; ladies in large flowered bonnets, light blouses and dark skirts walked beside the men or in groups of themselves in twos and threes.

On the northwest corner of Washington Place and Greene Street stood the Asch Building and the Triangle Shirtwaist Factory. She entered through a large double door with an ornate design carved on its front panel. On its windows in flowering gold letters were painted *The Asch Building* and its address. Inside the spacious foyer were several doors, each announcing in silver lettering various businesses. Kathleen also saw her first elevator. Never in a million years would she ride in one of those contraptions. What if the thing fell?

Not seeing the door for the Triangle Shirtwaist Company, she entered a small reception office off to her left. Inside the tiny smoke-filled room sat a squat, potbellied old man energetically grinding a cigar between his teeth. His pate was bald except for puffs of white hair growing around his huge ears. He looked up to see Kathleen enter and barely had time to ram a magazine out of sight before she reached his desk. She had glanced at an immodestly clad young woman on the cover.

Ignoring the growing flush in her cheeks from the shocking picture, she spoke politely. "I'm looking for the Triangle Shirtwaist Company. Can you tell me —"

His gravelly voice interrupted her. "Elevator's over there. Eighth and ninth floor for employment. Tenth for business." He looked away, dismissing her, obviously provoked by her intrusion.

"I don't care to take the elevator," she said meekly, trying not to further antagonize him.

"Stairs then. Down the hall." He jerked a stubby thumb in the general direction.

She quickly thanked him and hastened from his office.

"Damn females ought to go through the Employment Agency for Women," the man muttered peevishly. "Not be bothering me with them silly selves."

His abrupt rudeness followed Kathleen out the door, nearly reducing her to tears. As she turned down the hallway, she heard a loud snap as the man adjusted the magazine's pages.

"Sure, he's an ignoramus," she said, attempting to strengthen her flagging courage.

It was a little after five. She would get no work done today and perhaps not even be hired if she did not hustle. She found the stairway and rushed up the steps two at a time.

It unnerved her that she climbed continuously up

45

and up without reaching her floor. By the time she had hit the fifth landing, she was winded.

Her knees aching, she rested briefly, then again attacked the stairs. As she drew closer to her destination, a steady hum of noise reached her ears. At the eighth floor, the drone seemed as loud as the storm winds she had experienced at sea.

Pulling herself up the final steps with the handrail, she arrived at a door with *Triangle Shirtwaist Company* painted on a window protected by a wire mesh. She turned the knob. The door yielded heavily and closed slowly behind her.

Inside, the machines' monotonous sounds washed over her until she wanted to run. Then run, she scolded silently, or stay and do what you came here to do. You are an O'Donald. They never ran from a good fight in their lives. The men didn't and certainly, the women won't. Not this woman, anyway!

She shifted her coat from one arm to the other, adjusted her hat and brushed back a loose strand of hair. To her right was a small office. Unhesitatingly, she knocked for admittance.

A short, heavy man in baggy brown trousers and a rumpled white shirt waved her in. Smoke from a burning cigar circled his short cropped hair. His face was bathed in wrinkles. From out of his corrugated skin stared two icy-blue eyes. He scowled deeply, his face reminding Kathleen of a worm's body. He spoke gruffly, cigar ashes dribbling down his shirt.

"You looking for a job?"

She nodded wordlessly, his rough manner challenging her confidence.

"Answer me, lady, I ain't no mind reader. My name's Mr. Dobbs."

She hid a thick swallow in her throat. "Yes, Mr. Dobbs. I'm looking for a job."

"Irish, eh? We got five hundred workers at the Triangle. Mostly girls and mostly Russian Jews and Italians. Got some Poles, Germans, Hungarians, some Americans. Put you beside one of them. Can you run an electric sewing machine?"

She started to shake her head and remembered in time to speak. "No, but I sew a fine seam."

"Put you on hems for a while. You gotta learn the machines by Friday."

That was only three days away. "Isn't Friday awfully —"

He cut her off, his face folding in on itself. "Here's the rules: Work starts at seven in the morning. Pay's three dollars a week. Lunch is a half hour and if you buy it, it costs ten cents. It's dry cake, and you bring something to drink. We sell you needles at ten cents each, so mind you don't lose them. Electricity is extra when you get on the machines. You'll be given a quota to reach each day. You don't reach it, you stay till you finish. Work like hell here, and you'll do fine. Get caught talking too much and you're fired. Be on time every day or a floor boss'll be after your hide." He leered at her. "Nice hide, too. He won't mind a bit. Sometimes the bosses lets the girls off that way. Just don't let me catch you at it."

Kathleen's stomach churned. She wanted to run from Dobbs, from this place, from this country! To the devil with America.

Before she could tell him she had decided against working here, he had braced his effeminate hands against his desk and heaved himself out of his chair, indicating she should follow him.

She pursed her lips, remembering her earlier resolve that *this* O'Donald would not lose the fight. She ignored his crudeness and threats and fell in behind him.

In the large outer room, he said, "Hang your things in there."

Glancing inside the cloakroom, Kathleen saw dozens of hooks lining the walls, the workers' paraphernalia hanging from them. It did not strike her as a particularly safe place to leave the only coat she owned. Exiting, she said, "I'll keep my coat, if you don't mind."

Dobbs shrugged indifferently. "I'll put you next to Bertha Swartz," he said, making his way toward the middle of the room. "She's been here for years. She'll teach you the machine while you're hemming."

Good with figures and a critical observer, Kathleen quickly calculated that there were at least two hundred and forty machines which nearly filled the place. Sixteen parallel rows of long tables about seventy-five feet long held fifteen machines. At the opposite end of the room, the tables were backed against the far wall. She and Dobbs stood in the only aisle that gave exit to the cloakroom, toilets, two freight elevators and a fire escape. The tables were boarded from the floor to just below the table's surface, creating collection bins. Kathleen watched several women discard cloth scraps into these bins.

She assumed somebody eventually picked them up and perhaps used them to stuff pillows or children's dollies. Hanging on tiers above the workers were shirtwaists, which made the whole room look like a giant closet. Every two tables faced each other across a work trough which connected the tables. Beneath each trough ran a rotating axle which fed power to the machines. Just above the machine operator's knees was a wooden shell which caught the oil drippings. On the floor to each worker's right was a wicker basket stacked with the work she was to complete that day.

Kathleen, having just been through Ellis Island's rigorous processing, was distressed not so much by the compactness of the physical space of the factory as by the notice tacked above the machines warning workers not to read during working hours or during lunch. Not even allowed to read on their own time! She thought this was, indeed, a very strict place to work.

Only the row of tables closest to the opened windows, thick with dust and lint, saw any kind of natural light. And what did it matter anyway, Kathleen mused, the way the women were working. Toiling back to back, each one bent to her machine, her hands and fingers flying. Kathleen saw only the tops of heads; heads with hair parted in the middle, thick and thinly braided or piled high, hair of black, brown, white, or red, and, in spite of the heat, covered with brown or black wool scarves. Not a face did she see, not one pair of eyes.

The room was stuffy and she coughed. Even with

the windows opened, the ventilation was poor. The floor was covered with litter, cloth scraps, empty wooden spools and objects Kathleen could not identify.

Dobbs kicked aside a large pile of shirtwaist trimmings and cuttings. "Don't get caught using those freight elevators, neither. You're gonna get your pocketbook and pockets searched each night over by the door. Make sure you don't steal any shirtwaists. The girls here got sticky fingers. Had to fire two just last week."

Incensed that he would consider her capable of theft, she still took his warning seriously.

A man dressed much like Dobbs stopped nearby and loudly berated a woman who had apparently slowed her speed. "You hustle now, Maria. This ain't no vacation you're on." His face was heavily pitted from the pox and red from the room's high temperature. Full lips were set in a perturbed sneer. His deep-set eyes were hard, demanding. He, like Dobbs, smoked a cigar.

Maria visibly cringed beneath his words, and Kathleen noted a distinct quickening in her handling of the fine cloth speedily passing beneath the whirring needle of her machine. His grating, angry voice made a profound impression upon Kathleen. She vowed she would never incur his wrath.

"Mr. Howe," Dobbs said, pointing to the man. "He's one of the floor bosses. He keeps the girls working their best."

"He'll have no trouble from me, Mr. Dobbs." She was here to work and to get rich. Then she would travel to a finer place. Earlier today while still on Ellis Island, she had thought working in a factory might be fun. She would meet many people, make dozens of new friends, invite them to her home. She saw immediately that the Triangle was only a steppingstone for her. She would get out as soon as she could and go to someplace better, although she had no idea where that was just yet.

Reaching Bertha's machine, Dobbs said, "Bertha, show this girl — what's your name, girlie?"

"Kathleen O'Donald. I'm not a girl or a —"

"Show Kathy —"

"Kathleen, please."

But he seemed aware only of his own power as he looked disdainfully at her. His eyes became hard chunks of blue granite. "Show Kathy how to run your machine during lunch. She's gotta know by Friday."

Bertha's prominent cheekbones and sharp chin jutted forward as sweat ran down the sides of her face. Clear brown no-nonsense eyes looked Kathleen up and down. "And just when am I supposed to eat?" She was muscular, big and seemed quite bad-tempered. She wore her plain brown blouse rolled up at the sleeves. Her dark blue skirt was hiked up a bit to allow any moving air to cool her stockinged legs in this sweltering environment. An apron protected her clothing. Her thin salt-and-pepper hair was braided in tight plaits around her head. Her hands, surprisingly slender and graceful, fascinated Kathleen as she watched Bertha wave them angrily in the air, looking as though she were conducting a fine orchestra.

"Don't get sassy, girlie. Show her." Full of himself, he walked briskly, importantly away.

Kathleen started to apologize to Bertha.

"Forget it," Bertha snapped. "Just pull up a stool and sit down and watch. If you got any brains, maybe you can learn by looking, and I can have lunch every day. Won't be thirty minutes like it should. They wait till the girls ain't looking and then turn the clock up. We only really get twenty minutes. They think we don't know what they're up to, but we do. You know how much an extra ten minutes means to us?" She thrust her head in Dobbs's direction. "And to the owners of this joint? Big dollars for them. More work for us." She labored with quick, jerky movements, her graceful hands now trembling with rage. "We know, we do —"

"Shut up, Bertha. Get to work." From ten feet away, Howe stood glaring at her.

Bertha stopped talking and began operating her sewing machine, the needle making a rasping sound, sending cloth sailing beneath its tiny foot.

Kathleen pulled up a nearby stool, amazed that Bertha would complain about her bosses to a total stranger. She had to be bitter, indeed.

Kathleen folded her coat, placed it on the stool and made herself comfortable. She sat between Bertha to her right and a tiny slip of a woman to her left, whose hair was the color of copper and whose eyes were as blue as a cloudless Antrim day. She was as tired-looking as Kathleen had ever seen a body look.

The woman whispered, "My name is Mary." She spoke with a heavy Italian accent, and it took Kathleen a couple of seconds to decipher what she had said.

"How do you do? I'm Kathleen."

As Mary smiled, years fell away from her face. It jolted Kathleen to realize that Mary was a young woman.

A lanky man with a handsome face spoiled by insolent eyes stopped alongside her. He wore a soiled white shirt and disheveled black trousers. In his arms, he carried a large stack of unfinished shirtwaists. Unceremoniously, he dumped them in the basket next to Kathleen. "I'm Phil Jamison. I'm a floor boss, here. This is a third of what you'll do each day. You're only getting this much work since you came in real late today. They're due by closing."

Incredulously, Kathleen said, "I don't know . . ."

His toneless stare thwarted her protest. "Closing," he snapped, and walked away.

Seconds later, she heard him sweet-talking a lovely young woman seated several stools down from Kathleen. His face had softened, and the woman was smiling. They were obviously interested in each other.

Kathleen faced the pile of fabric beside her, and her heart sank. "I don't even know what I'm supposed to do."

"Here," Bertha said impatiently. "You're going to be hemming cuffs and along the waist. I'll at least get you started. You'll be up all night as it is."

"All night? When exactly is closing?" Bertha snatched a shirtwaist from Kathleen's basket and reached for a needle stuck in her apron. Deftly, she threaded the eye from a white spool of thread she pulled from her pocket as Kathleen repeated, "When is closing? Mr. Jamison just said this is only a third of a day's work. What do you mean, I'll be up all night?"

"Listen, dearie . . ."

"Kathleen."

"Oh, don't be so uppity," Bertha rejoined. "This is a half-day's work, only he didn't tell you because he wants a half-day's work out of you for a fifth of a day's pay."

Kathleen felt her face grow warm with anger. "I don't have to stand for this. Who may I complain to?"

Bertha snorted, the closest that Kathleen would ever hear her come to laughing. "You got a complaint, take it to Mr. Dobbs, and it's been real nice knowing you." She tossed the shirtwaist aside, turned back to her machine and began madly sewing.

So, Kathleen thought, it's like that, is it? Give her a half-day's work would they? She picked up the shirtwaist. "Show me, Bertha. Quickly."

Bertha snorted again and in seconds, Kathleen was duplicating the tiny neat stitches her impatient teacher had shown her. Now her head was down; now her back was bent except for occasional glances to observe Bertha's task.

For the next two hours, Kathleen toiled without speaking. By then her back ached so badly she could barely stand it and had taken to leaning her elbows against the table and sewing with the shirtwaist in front of her instead of on her lap. It was less speedy sewing this way, but she could no longer sit up straight on the beastly stool which had no back support. She continued to cough as well, presumably from the lint she could see floating in the air. She was so used to being outdoors that breathing this air seemed much like inhaling chunks of dirt.

Yet she was thankful to be seated away from the windows. She did not relish the idea of being high enough in the sky to watch hundreds of pigeons sail through the city. She did not even want to think about all the people stacked beneath her. She shuddered at the idea that she sat on top of someone's head every time they walked beneath her stool. It did not matter that she could not see them nor hear them. She knew they were down there, and that was enough.

She attempted to comfort herself with thoughts of Ireland, and as she sewed, she envisioned her lovely green country. It rained two days out of three, and it was always damp, but it had been her home.

She felt a tear start to swell and heard, "Cryin' ain't gonna do you a lick of good, Kathy, so just keep sewing so's you can go home by ten or eleven. It ain't good to cry. You need your strength to finish that pile there."

Embarrassed by Bertha's straightforwardness, Kathleen sniffed away her tears. She ignored the hunger pangs in her belly that had been nagging her for hours and inhaled deeply as her determined fingers picked up speed. She coughed again and ignored that, too.

A sudden hush within the large room drew her attention. Dozens of women shut off their machines and rose, chatting and laughing amongst themselves. They collected their belongings, underwent Mr.

Dobbs's quick inspection of their pocketbooks and pockets and headed out the door that Kathleen, seemingly centuries ago, had passed through. It was only seven P.M.

Bertha and Mary were also preparing to leave. Bertha leaned close to Kathleen. "Keep pluggin' like that, and you'll be done in a couple of hours." From beneath a stack of fabric, she pulled out a big black pocketbook and joined the others.

Mary bid Kathleen a pleasant good night. Kathleen nodded, shocked again at how young Mary looked when she smiled and how very old she seemed when bent over her machine.

With the noise cut down, Kathleen could hear the women's heavy leather shoes clumping down the stairs, hear their laughter. From afar, their voices bounced off the walls of the stairwell in languages Kathleen did not understand.

She wondered where they were all headed, where they lived, what they did for fun or if, as exhausted as she was, they went straight home to bed. That's what she would do, were she free to leave. She could hardly believe she had left the ship only this morning, found a place to live and was already working in a single day's time.

This is America, she thought. Here is where things happen. She could do this task and be out of there by ten. It would take her that long, but she could do it and do a good job, too. This was America.

She lowered her eyes to the shirtwaist before her and firmly and swiftly pushed the needle through the cloth. With her mind only on completing the mountain of work still sitting beside her, she slipped and painfully stabbed herself. She flinched but did not cry out. She sucked the blood until it stopped flowing and concentrated even harder on her needlework. If anything, she increased her speed.

"This is America," she whispered, blinking back determined tears.

CHAPTER FIVE

Tuesday, July 13, 1909

At ten P.M., Kathleen stopped working. There were a few other women still sweating over their machines. All were extremely young, probably not older than seventeen. Well, they could stay; she had had enough, and she was leaving, no matter what. She was faint with hunger and hoped the Solinskis had something she could eat when she got back to their apartment.

She stood and arched her back to ease tight muscles causing her spasms of pain. She was envious of Rose who, no doubt at this moment, slept peacefully in the loft of a beautiful home as was the custom of servants who worked for the rich.

As she passed them by, those still toiling never paused, never slowed, but kept busily working, their hands flying, their eyes glued to their piecework.

After having made sure Bertha's needle was safely wrapped in a piece of cloth tucked deep in her pocket, she picked up her coat from the stool and made her way toward the door. The poor lighting in the place from the glaring bulbs hanging down had tired her eyes terribly. She rubbed them a bit as she reached for the doorknob.

Mr. Jamison appeared as if from nowhere. He braced his hand firmly against the door. "Where to, girlie?"

His scowl was as fierce as ever. How could a man this handsome be so frightening? She was determined he would not intimidate her; her eyes locked on his. "I'm going home. It's late and I can't work anymore tonight."

He did not remove his hand from the door as he took a step closer to her, causing her to move back. "I been watching you all evening, girlie. You ain't finished. You ain't even near finished."

"I was given a half-day's work," she countered angrily. "Not a third of a day's work as I was told. I can't possibly finish it. I've done more than my share today."

Jamison thoughtfully pursed thin lips. "Smart aleck, ain't you? You ain't gonna last long here."

She wiped away a bead of sweat ready to fall from the tip of her nose. "Then I won't. There are other factories. I'll always find work."

"Not if I send your name around, you won't." Jamison smiled with cruel, chilling confidence.

"I don't understand."

"I'll have you blacklisted, girlie, and you won't get work in this city, or anyplace else that has your name. Now you get back there and finish up. You ain't got but about two more hours to go. So hop to it."

Kathleen did not need to have "blacklisted" explained to her. She turned to go back to her seat, and as she did, Jamison lightly smacked her bottom. She whirled on him to slap him, but he was ready for her and grasped her hand as it flew toward his face.

"You could be fired on the spot for that, girlie, or you could be excused from all that work and do a couple of hours with me. That'd get you out of it."

"You shame me, sir, you shame me!" She fought rage; she fought tears; she fought the urge to attack and kill him. "I'd work forever before I'd have anything to do with the scummy likes of you. You, sir, shall be reported first thing tomorrow morning."

He threw back his head and laughed. A breath loaded with the scent of garlic hit her in the face, nauseating her. "Likely Dobbs'll laugh himself sick, girlie, and bed you himself." His face changed from devilish merriment to blatant hostility. "Now get back to your bench."

She did not argue. She would lose. She did not want to lose. She did not want to forfeit her job, her self-respect, her dignity. Arrogantly, she returned to her work as if she were Ireland's queen and he nothing more than a lowly knave due to get his head hacked off at sunrise.

He was right about how much longer she would be here. She completed the last shirtwaist by midnight, and this time when she reached the exit door, he briefly inspected her pockets, then let her pass.

His impertinent eyes followed her. She felt her clothing being ripped away piece by piece with his penetrating gaze. Ignoring the stifling room, she quickly drew on her coat and wrapped her arms around herself as she made her way down the dark stairs. She was afraid now, afraid of him, afraid of the hour. Never before had she been out alone this late.

The streets were nearly deserted. There were a few men about and fewer lone women hastening toward some unknown destination. "If you're smart, lassies," she whispered, "you'll get home and tuck yourselves safe into bed as soon as you can."

She too hurried along, her footsteps echoing off the buildings. Some factories were still operating; others were dark and deserted. She was glad she did not have far to walk, run actually, as her speed steadily increased and she glanced from side to side and from front to rear.

She saw a policeman as she hurried by. He politely tipped his hat. "Evening, miss." He spoke seemingly musically. He flooded her mind with thoughts of home, beautiful men and women's voices blending in harmony in her church, the sounds of lowing cows begging to be milked morning and evening, the smell of the horses as she combed their sleek coats. She became so homesick she thought she would not be able to take another step forward. Only the policeman's being a stranger pushed her on. An officer of the law or not, she was alone, and he was big!

"Evening to you, sir," she answered, polite yet cautious, slowing her pace not a whit.

Hastening after her, he said, "You must be a lass not long from home." By streetlight, Kathleen could see that under his blue uniform and cap, he was quite a thin fellow, with eyes buried beneath dense black eyebrows and a large toothy grin obscured by a flamboyant handlebar moustache. His charming smile allowed her to relax a bit. She recognized that the terrible tiredness within her own body and mind had made her afraid of all living things right now.

"Off the ship today, sir," she replied rather breathlessly. "County Antrim."

"Here now, miss, slow down," he said, catching up to her. "I'll walk you to your door. There's ragamuffins about that'd sooner steal the gold from your teeth as look at you."

She was so grateful for his kind offer, she could have cried. But she did not. She was through with being a tearful, homesick woman — at least for this day. "I would appreciate it, Officer."

"Me name's Patrick Shawnery," he said, "from County Fermanagh five years ago this very month. Are you just getting out of the factory?"

"I am," she answered. "The Triangle. They worked me awfully hard today."

"They work everybody hard, from children twelve, fourteen years old to old women who should be rocking their bairn on their knees and waiting for the good Lord to take them away. Not the bairns, mind you. Just their old rickety selves. But there they are up in those sweatshops —"

"Sweatshops?"

"That's what they're called, miss. Sweatshops. It's a factory or a home or any hole in the wall where you work for slave wages and sweat your life away doing it."

"Sweatshops." Kathleen contemplated the word. "Sure, it seems that you're right, Officer Shawnery. I sweat a lot today while I worked."

His friendly manner was infectious. She felt much better than she had since walking into the factory seven hours ago.

They turned onto Wooster Street. "I live over there," she said. He followed her across the street and to her door. "I thank you, Officer Shawnery . . ."

"Just Patrick will do, miss."

His broad smile again lifted her spirits. "I'm sure that I was kept safe by your presence."

"I'll keep me eyes peeled for you hereafter, lass. You'll be safe on me beat."

She said goodnight and let herself into the main hall. The city smells of gasoline, horse manure and factory smoke were left behind as she entered the building. In exchange, she was again struck with the stench of urine and this evening's meals potent with the scent of garlic. Something scurried across her foot. She screeched and leaped toward the stairs leading to her apartment.

Even in the dark, her fear of whatever creature it was that had just touched her — a rat, a cat, a small dog, and deep in her heart she knew it was a rat — sharpened her memory, and in the dim light of the hallway gas lamp she had no trouble locating her apartment.

She breathed a great sigh of relief as she gripped the door handle and turned. Locked! Not having been given a key, she tried again in the hopes that the door was merely stuck. But it was not. The thought of knocking filled her with dread. She had seen earlier how exhausted the family looked, and she hated to disturb them. She considered going downstairs and rousing Grace, but then she remembered how frightful the landlady was, so she chose instead to wake someone within the apartment.

She knocked tentatively. With no response, she knocked louder a second time. Still nothing happened. "Are they dead to the world?" she whispered. She tried yet again and was rewarded, but from the apartment across the hall. The door opened and an angry male voice hissed, "Quit your damn banging. There's people trying to sleep."

"I can't get in, and I live here," she whispered back.

"Then get yourself a damn key, and quit bothering the rest of us." He violently slammed his door, and that did the trick.

Benjamin opened his door, hiking up the suspenders to his trousers. A lamp burned dimly on the table. "It's you, Kathleen. We don't like loose women here. You can't stay here anymore. We don't like fast women. Coming in late like this. The nerve." In spite of his accent, she clearly understood him. He started to close the door in her face.

"No," she cried. "I'm just getting home from work.

And I am *not* a fast woman. How dare you! Now you let me in so's I can go to bed." She pushed past him, into the room. Her bed was covered with articles of clothing. In frenzied hysteria, she scooped them up and hurled them to the floor saying, "This is my bed. Do you understand? Mine! I rented it, and I will sleep in it. Use it as a table during the day if you wish, but when I come home at night, at whatever hour, it is to be cleared of debris." Without undressing, she threw herself down and angrily punched her coat into what passed for a pillow. With her first paycheck, she would get a proper pillow.

She drew a moldy-smelling blanket up around her chin and heard Sadie shifting in bed. Sasha called out once, and Benjamin spoke soothingly to her. Kathleen was not yet sure where the girl was sleeping, but it was not far from herself.

Benjamin said, "I'm sorry, Kathleen, for having insulted you. The last lady who stayed here was a bad woman. I thought with your coming in so late . . ."

"Well, you thought wrong. I'm a good Christian woman. A Catholic. Roman!"

"And I'm a good Catholic, too," he said. "Polish."

Penitent, she said, "I'm sure you are, sir. I'm just overwhelmed by this day. We'll talk in the morning. Now, goodnight to you."

"Goodnight, Kathleen. We rise at four-thirty."

Despair swept over her. She would have to get up in four hours. In addition, she was sleeping on soapboxes and in her *clothing*. Her parents would have fits if they knew. Likely, too, they would squirm in their graves regarding her potential new friends. Before she ever quit the factory, most of them were apt to be Jews, Italians, Poles, Germans and very few Irish.

Tired as she was, she mulled over her situation. Benjamin seemed pleasant enough. He had apologized for having called her a fast woman. He had a family, and all of them hard-working people, including the little girl, Sasha.

As she allowed her muscles to relax, Kathleen began to feel somewhat safe for the first time today. If anything, the Solinskis were in danger from her. She had wanted to kill a man tonight.

She dozed off saying her prayers while listening to rats traveling through the walls and the rumblings of her empty stomach.

At first, she thought she had been awakened by an obnoxious fly crawling across her nose and lips. But then she felt a small hand on her shoulder. Sasha was speaking to her in Polish. In a barely understandable accent, Kathleen heard Sadie say, "My daughter can't speak English. She's trying to tell you it's time to get up." Sadie steered Sasha from Kathleen's bedside. "Breakfast will be in fifteen minutes."

Breakfast! As hungry as Kathleen was, she had just laid down. She did not think she had the strength to rise. She said, "Please wake me at six," and rolled toward the wall.

"Breakfast is in fifteen minutes," Sadie repeated, sternly this time.

At some time while Kathleen slept, the clothing she had flung to the floor had been picked up. A blanket had been temporarily strung across a wire near her bed giving her privacy in which to dress. A chamber pot had also been placed nearby, but she would use the facilities down the hall. My word, she thought, using a chamber pot with so many strangers about.

After having slept in them, she straightened her clothes, then smoothed her bed. On her way out to the bathroom, she saw Sasha return to her sleeping area. It was nothing but a hole she had burrowed out of a stack of coat pieces.

In the hallway near the bathroom door, a gas light burned. Several people, in varying degrees of dress, waited in line before her. Although she made an attempt at friendly conversation, no one returned her kindness. Having failed at that, she leaned against the wall as most of them did and closed her eyes.

Lord, she prayed, *in twenty-four hours your daughter has changed from knowing nothing to knowing too much, and none of it good. Please help me make it through this day without quitting my job. I want to be better than that, stronger than that. Thank you for listening to my brief prayer because honestly, Lord, I haven't the strength to say more.*

Eventually her turn came. Although the bathroom had hot water and the added luxury of a claw-footed tub, the room was uncomfortably cluttered with other people's used towels, soiled clothing and shaving gear. How could people live like this? Didn't they care about themselves? About anything?

She spent little time in the bathroom before returning to the apartment. The Solinskis were already seated at the table, their heads bowed, their hands joined together. Candlelight flickered across their faces. They looked exceedingly tired.

They had set a place for her. She blessed herself and said grace.

Kathleen smiled directly at Sasha and said, "Your name is lovely, Sasha. I like it very much. My name is Kathleen."

Sadie translated, and Sasha grinned broadly. She pointed to a corner of the room at what Kathleen assumed was merely another bundle of clothing.

As Sasha spoke, Sadie explained, "Ruth and Irving are asleep in the clothes. They're twins."

It was difficult for Kathleen not to gasp in unpleasant surprise or burst into tears. More children here? And babies at that, sleeping amongst clothing because there were not enough beds! Clearly there was no money with which to buy even one! Was Kathleen sleeping in Sasha's bed? In the babies'?

Exercising steel control, she walked over to see the infants. They were not more than three months old. They slept soundly and seemed warm and content, their eyes fluttering and rolling back and forth beneath milky eyelids. Sadie must have risen some time ago to breast feed them before getting breakfast on the table.

Kathleen said, "Your children are beautiful."

They ate bread and cheese and drank water. Kathleen could have devoured all the food in sight, but she ate only what was put on her plate. She would be famished by lunch time.

Breakfast was concluded when every dish was washed and put away and the little ones rediapered and tucked back into their makeshift cradle.

With an hour and a half before she had to be at

work, Kathleen sat on her bed and took a more critical look at her first home in this country.

The narrow apartment allowed a severe argument to be heard through paper-thin walls. Light was beginning to struggle through filthy outside windows not yet opened in the early morning hours. Overhead, several wires criss-crossed the room. From them hung completed garments ready for Sasha to press, a task for which she was already preparing, the flat iron heating on the stove, the ironing board set up close to the window. Kathleen's blanket had been removed and finished articles of clothing hung on the wire.

Sadie picked up several pieces of clothing from here and there and carefully laid them out on the double bed. She explained to Kathleen, "I need your bed now to lay out the work we must do in the next hour so that there is not a moment wasted searching for it."

Reluctantly, Kathleen moved to the table, feeling in the way and of no use at all. She said to Sadie, "May I wash the windows for you?"

Sadie's gratitude embarrassed Kathleen. "That would be very nice."

Afterward, the early morning light streaming through the clean glass was considerable. If she stayed here, Kathleen decided, she would keep the windows sparkling as her personal chore.

By the time she had completed the tiny job, the Solinskis were working as fast as their hands could move.

The babies began to fuss, and, again, Kathleen made herself helpful by playing with them and changing their diapers. Twins! God help this family. They did not need twins. For that matter, they did not need any children in their present situation. But children came with marriage.

Kathleen looked at Sasha. It was conceivable that in five or six years this young child could have a husband and children. Kathleen cringed at the thought. In Ireland, there were very young brides, but they went to real homes, not hovels like this one.

At six-thirty, she left for work feeling guilty for all the time she had sat doing nothing while the Solinskis toiled like machines. She would like to have helped them, but she did not dare spend the energy. She knew what kind of a day she had ahead of her, and she must conserve every ounce of strength for that task.

Checking her pocket to be sure Bertha's needle and her own money were carefully tucked away, she picked up her coat, bid good-day to the Solinskis and let herself out of the apartment.

CHAPTER SIX
Wednesday, July 14, 1909

Her knees aching, Kathleen reached the eighth floor and turned the Triangle's doorknob. The machines' abrasive noise again struck her, and she wondered if she would ever become accustomed to such racket. Fearing her coat would be stolen, she kept it with her, intending to sit on it once more.

From his office door, Dobbs offhandedly waved his cigar at her indicating she should return to yesterday's station. It surprised and unsettled her to find everyone already hard at work, as though they had been there for several hours.

She had no sooner seated herself when Jamison, the floorwalker who had heaped such a load of shirtwaists on her yesterday, threw a pile in her basket again, today. She closed her eyes in dismay and gritted her teeth. Today's work seemed ten times greater.

"By seven tonight," he growled. He strolled over to the woman he had spoken to so pleasantly yesterday. He had stopped by her several times, each time the woman smiling at him. They whispered intimately together before he walked on.

So the man had feelings, but not toward Kathleen. She barely breathed, "By seven. I'll never make it."

Bertha, her machine already a whir of sound, snorted. "You'll make it or take it home."

"Sure, and it'll be impossible to finish. Why do they push me so?"

Bertha snatched a partially completed shirtwaist from her machine, quickly inspected it and passed it to the woman on her right. She picked up another and began sewing. Her efficient use of motion made her hands look as though they danced. She flinched and stopped a moment to flex them.

"Damn, I'm beginning to get a lot of pain in my wrists. Don't know what to make of it." She began sewing again. "To answer your question. They push you to make rich bastards richer. The hundreds of shirtwaists we make here that earn us three or four or five dollars a week will bring in hundreds of dollars in the wealthy ladies' shops."

"Three dollars a week? Only three?" Kathleen sat as if carved of granite.

"Beginners start at three," Bertha said, unaware of the shockwaves she had sent coursing through Kathleen's body. "The women who've been here the longest are getting six, maybe seven dollars, but they're few and far between. You can bet your sweet little fanny they don't tell anybody who they are, or they'd be picked on till they couldn't stand it."

Kathleen never heard her. Three dollars a week. Why had she not remembered yesterday what the wages were? She should quit now, *right* now, and go to another factory.

Her hopes disintegrated as Bertha said, "That's about the going rate around New York, Philadelphia, Chicago." She leaned toward Kathleen, her eyes never leaving her machine. "There's meetings going on."

"Meetings?" Kathleen glanced at Bertha, her mind still on her scant wages.

"Secret meetings," Bertha whispered. "Some of the girls are sick of working for shit. They want more. There's talk going around —"

"Hurry up, you two." Howe, the other floorwalker, stood behind them. "Bertha, you know better than to be gabbing. Kathy, get your needle out and start sewing or start walking. Make up your mind, girlie."

As he walked off, Kathleen reached into her pocket. Her hands shook so, she could barely open the cloth holding the tiny needle and found it nearly impossible to thread. Mr. Howe need not have hollered so. Quietly speaking to her would have been quite enough. Tears stung her eyes and blurred her vision, making her beginning stitches difficult to see.

From the side of her mouth, Bertha sternly whispered, "Quit your tears, Kathy. They see that and they'll make life tougher on you. You gotta be stronger than they are."

Kathleen nodded, swiftly wiping her eyes on her sleeve. When lunch rolled around she would ask Bertha about those meetings. She was unsure if she wanted to become involved in secret meetings, but if it meant better pay, maybe she could just see what was going on without being drawn in.

At lunch time she had neither the opportunity to talk to Bertha nor to spend time with her. At noon when most everyone else had stopped their machines, Kathleen considered her remaining day's work. She was not yet halfway through, but if she skipped lunch, she might catch up with herself and finish by seven. Anyway, she was no longer sure she could afford a dime a day for lunch. Three dollars! An impossible salary to live on. Dispirited, she picked up another shirtwaist.

Unmercifully driving herself all day, she tucked away Bertha's needle at seven sharp. Leaving the building, Bertha caught up with her. "Just a tip, girlie. Be here well before seven, and you don't have to work so fast. Most of the girls are here by six. That way they can do more and make more money if they're on piecework. They don't have to work quite so fast if they're not. You gotta be careful about working so fast like you been doing. The bosses catch on to that and they'll give you more work just because you came in early. And if you ain't on piecework, you're gonna do a whole lot of work for nothing. Think it over."

She started to move on as Kathleen asked, "What about the meetings, Bertha?"

"*Shut up*," Bertha hissed. She gave Kathleen a withering look. "I told you, they're secret. You wanna know more, you ask when we ain't around here. God, they'll have my ass." She quickly distanced herself from Kathleen. Other women brushed past her. In seconds she was alone.

"Evening, miss." Officer Patrick stood beside her. "A fine night." He looked toward the smoky, gray sky, its endless space blocked by large buildings fouling the air.

"I suppose it is," she said. She sighed and started walking.

Patrick strolled along with her. "I think I hear a bit of sadness in your voice this evening."

"Aye, I'm sad. I don't like my job. In fact, I hate it and I've only worked here a day and a half."

"Sure, and it's a job to hate," he agreed. "That's why I'm a member of New York City's finest and not slaving away in one of these stinking factories. Me mother works in one. She hates it, too."

"Then why does she do it?" Kathleen fought tears for a second time today, loathing herself for being so weak.

"Money. That's the only reason. And not much money, either. But it puts bread on the table. I've got a wife and a wee one. Between me mother and meself, we make ends meet."

"Well, I'm glad for you, Officer Patrick. I'm glad someone's making it. I'm frightened about my salary. It won't be much, maybe not even enough to pay my room and board."

"It's a tough city, lass, that's true, but you stick to your knitting and you'll do just fine. Don't let them get to you."

Kathleen kicked aside a tin can. "It's hard."

Patrick nodded, and Kathleen was happy for his quiet understanding and protection as he accompanied her again tonight.

A good Irish boy, she thought, and was instantly overwhelmed with chest-aching homesickness.

She remained at the Solinskis, unwilling to face the challenge of hunting for another apartment. They were kind to her, and she had become attached to their bairn.

For the next four weeks, she made thousands of stitches for the Triangle Shirtwaist Company. She was never put on a sewing machine, but sat beside Bertha and worked on stacks of shirtwaists and then worked on stacks more.

Following Bertha's suggestion, Kathleen had come in an hour, then an hour and a half, and finally two hours early. She could pace herself better, and it allowed her a lunch break.

She found, however, that the longer hours were devastating to her bladder. She began to drink less fluids so that she would not have to use the toilet room. The place was filthy, with no paper to dry herself and no water with which to wash her hands, just a toilet feculent and flyblown. Suffering through hours of discomfort until she reached home was far better than using these facilities. As a result, she became dehydrated and more and more tired.

The backless stool was also taking its toll. As she worked, she tried numerous ways of sitting or half-standing or leaning on the table before her.

Relief lasted only minutes before shifting to a new position became necessary. Yet, to do anything but sew as fast as one could was to invite a good scolding. The floor bosses made sure their voices carried well above any rattling machines so that other workers took a lesson from some poor humiliated woman's forgetfulness.

The dirt and clutter covering the factory floor vexed Kathleen's sense of cleanliness and order. And, like all the other factory hirelings, she coughed steadily, she guessed, from inhaling airborne lint for thirteen, fourteen and sometimes fifteen hours a day.

So far she had received only three dollars for three weeks' work. Her first week's salary was never given to her; Dobbs claimed it was a training week. The second week saw an automatic withdrawal of three dollars for any damages to shirtwaists which she might incur. The week before, however, she had finally been given her full three dollars. In a few days, her rent would be due. After using part of this week's and all of last week's salary to pay it, she hoped to able to get ahead. Ahead of what, she wondered as she picked up another shirtwaist.

She was so tired today that she thought she fell asleep once, but she was not sure. Thinking she was imagining things, she kept sewing as if nothing strange had happened. Needle in, needle out, needle in, needle out. She operated automatically, barely thinking and barely moving except to ease her aching back. She had become like all the other women — head down, back bent, uncommunicative, concentrating only on the task before her so that she could finish by seven if possible, go home, eat a meal of black beans, cheese and bread and fall into bed until four-thirty the following morning when she would help with the twins, have breakfast and return to work. She herself had become a machine.

She did not know what possessed her, then, to break for a moment, to risk wasting time and incurring the venom of Mr. Howe or Mr. Jamison. But she was angry. Her woman's time was upon her, and she felt worse than usual. Defiantly, she stood and stretched, eyeing the rows of women working. No one yelled at her, no one came near her. She heaved a relieved sigh then caught her breath. On the far side of the room was a vaguely familiar form. Could it possibly be? Kathleen blinked to ease her aching eyes and looked again. Rose! Rose sitting and working as if she had been there all her life.

Dumbfounded, Kathleen returned to her sewing, occasionally glancing Rose's way, but not once did Rose raise her eyes. Kathleen willed Rose to look up. Still Rose worked on. Why had the Englishwoman not spoken to her, let her know she was here, met her at lunch or after work? She knew that Kathleen was going to apply for a position at the Triangle.

"Kathy!"

She jumped guiltily.

"Come 'ere!"

From a couple of tables away, Howe waved to her. She set down her sewing, being careful to take her needle with her.

"You're going on a machine this morning. Over this way."

Obediently, she followed him to the far reaches of the room. She glanced toward Rose who was oblivious to all except the shirtwaist in her lap.

"The woman who ran this machine got married

and quit. Watch me and take over." Howe sat down and with surprising skill demonstrated how to stitch the hem around the bottom of a shirtwaist. "I'll be around later to check on you. Anything not done right is gonna be ripped out and done over."

The brief instructions completed, she sat and began to sew. She fought to control her shaking hands as Howe stood behind her, leaning slightly over her with the possessive air of an English overlord.

She had observed Bertha many times and thought she could easily do the job. But thinking about running a machine and actually doing it was a trying challenge. It was difficult to keep the cloth moving at an even pace. There would be several shirtwaists to redo before this day was through, she thought. But being on a machine was reward enough for ripping out a few mistakes. She was seated on a lower stool, instantly giving her back some relief. Not much, she realized, but some rest was better than what she had been suffering for weeks.

Howe grumbled but did not speak to her. Eventually he left, and she did indeed improve. She was not fast, but her accuracy improved after she had completed several dozen pieces. Howe returned a half hour later and picked out fourteen articles he wanted redone. Not too bad, she thought, considering what she had already accomplished.

Hours later, her back ached as viciously as ever. In addition, she had been so tense that the calves of her legs had painful knots in them. No matter how she flexed her feet and legs, she could not ease her discomfort. She bit her lip, ignoring her plight, knowing that to be on a machine was to earn more money. Coughing, her legs throbbing, her eyes stinging, she worked steadily on, not talking to her new neighbors, her mind not even registering who they were or what they looked like. Shirtwaist after shirtwaist, she sewed for seven and a half solid hours.

At seven P.M., she had not completed her quota. Jamison stopped at her side. "You've done well today. Be here early in the morning and finish up so that you can finish tomorrow's work on time."

She nodded exhaustedly, grateful that he seemed to have a wondrously generous side to him this evening. She picked up her coat and made her way to the door.

At the last minute, she remembered Rose. She scanned the rows, looking for her. And suddenly, there she was, gazing back at her, a big smile plastered across her face. She did not look up long, but the smile stayed with her as she returned to her work. To Rose's left was a stack of shirtwaists as high as if she had just begun her workday.

Sweatshop, Kathleen thought. The Triangle's that, all right. She wondered what time Rose would finish and briefly considered waiting for her. No, it would be hours before Rose could leave.

Kathleen made her way home, her thoughts on Rose, the woman she had once hated because she was from England.

Nearing Wooster Street, she said her evening prayers so that when she got into bed, she could go directly to sleep. She was concerned she no longer prayed on her knees and had not since she had fallen asleep twice while kneeling at her bedside. She had slipped sideways and made an awful racket.

Sadie was at her side in an instant. Kathleen claimed she had fallen out of bed. She felt criminal for lying and guilty for no longer daring to kneel. Praying on the way home seemed the best choice. Otherwise, her prayers would never be completed, not even the Lord's Prayer, the one she always said first.

Thankfully, Sadie had told her of St. Joseph's Church on Washington Place. She had to cross beneath the Sixth Avenue elevated train to get there, which terrified her, and its awful racket during service was a terrible distraction and annoyance. But Father Michael's booming voice saying the Latin mass never failed to steady and soothe her spirit.

CHAPTER SEVEN
Wednesday, August 11, 1909

A month had passed and there had been no opportunity to meet with Rose. Rose did not take lunch, working straight through. Kathleen would like to have waited for her at the end of a day but could not bear the thought of tarrying. She always hurt and was so tired that she wanted only to collapse into bed until the morrow. Perhaps on Saturday evening they could go somewhere for tea.

Since first meeting Rose, Kathleen had changed, reluctantly letting go of the Ireland-England feud. It was not because of the words Rose had left with Kathleen weeks ago while on board ship — "We are going to a new country for new battles" — but because Rose continued to smile warmly at her day after day.

Rose looked terrible, no longer the brave woman willing to face Ellis Island alone if need be, with Kathleen if Kathleen would allow it. She appeared exhausted, stooped and like all the others, she frequently coughed.

On Saturday as Kathleen stilled her machine and put her things neatly away, she ignored her personal malaise, keeping her commitment to meet Rose. It had been a cool day. Perhaps the normally baking sidewalks and stone and brick buildings would be merciful as she waited. Rose had hours of sewing ahead of her.

Their smiles met somewhere mid-room as Kathleen left with several women. Once outside, the rest moved on, chatting about going dancing or dining. Kathleen wondered where they got the strength. She assumed they were out to catch a man and free themselves of the life they led. She herself had considered it since the third week of working at the Triangle.

She hurried to church for confession and was back at the factory in less than half an hour.

Patrick sauntered by and saw her lingering at the door. Tipping his hat, he asked, "Need an escort tonight?"

"I'm waiting for a friend," she answered. She

pulled her coat a little tighter around her neck, hoping she had not missed Rose. That was a possibility too.

"It's a bit of a nip tonight," he said. "Don't wait too long. You'll catch your death."

His kindness warmed her. "Thank you, Patrick."

He smiled and moved off. She knew he would hang about until Rose showed or Kathleen left, considerate of the factory girls on his beat.

Two hours passed before another group emerged from the building. Among them, thank the Blessed Mother, was Rose. She did not notice Kathleen until she spoke. "Hello, Rose."

"Kathleen!"

"I waited for you."

After a brief hug, Rose said, "I see. Well, and I'm glad you did. How wonderful to see you again. You look grand!"

It was a lie, and they both knew it. Rose looked like walking death, and each had lost weight and color and energy, in spite of their radiant smiles.

"I thought," Kathleen said, blushing, "if it was all right with you, we might take a cup of tea." She had saved out two dimes from her scant earnings this week and felt the pressure of even that little bit.

She was ecstatic to be doing something different. Since coming to America, she had spent every Saturday night at home, with the exception of her weekly confessions when she spent a few minutes alone with Father Michael who sat hidden in his darkened confessional chamber listening to her whispered sins. She had been cranky to a neighbor; she had said "damn" three times; she hadn't gotten up on time for the past three days in a row. She was *bored*!

Rose nodded. "I could use a coffee. Two, in fact." Two? Kathleen clutched the dimes in her pocket.

"I'll treat us to the second cup if you want another," Rose offered.

Kathleen released the dimes and withdrew her hand. "That would be nice, but my limit is one cup before bedtime."

"I only live a block from here," Rose said as they walked toward Crosby and Prince Streets. On the corner, a two-story clapboard building with a storefront facing Prince Street, greeted them. Feeling the rounded cobblestones through the thin leather soles of her shoes, Kathleen crossed the street and entered the Crosby side entrance. At the rear of the store and separate from it, was a popular small coffeeshop simply called Ellie's that catered to late night factory workers.

"Smells good in here," Rose said, as the door closed behind them. Like friendly arms, warmth from the day's baking wrapped itself around Kathleen.

They sat in a wooden booth opposite the counter. Women from nearby factories filled the seats, some with men, others in groups laughing, and, Kathleen noticed, a couple of women crying. Politely, she ignored them.

"How do you come to be at the Triangle of all places?" Kathleen asked after they had given their orders.

"I knew you were there. If I could get meself into that factory, then I could start out knowing at least one person. Trouble is, they gave me so much work for the first two weeks I couldn't even look up to watch you leave each day. In fact, I didn't even know you'd left. Too tired. Hurt too much. I'm better now and can pay more attention to what's going on including knowing that you're around." Rose's face changed from a lovely smile to a heavy cloud. Her voice became low and angry. "I didn't want factory work. I'm not very damn good at it, but I didn't know what else to do. The mistress, she wouldn't recommend another house to me. She was very angry that I chose to leave since me work was impeccable. But . . ." She leaned toward Kathleen. "The house has two young men, boys really. They're feeling their oats. It was them or me."

"I see," Kathleen answered noncommittally, stunned that Rose had been so little respected. They were brought tea and coffee. Kathleen liberally laced her tea with cream and sugar. "It's a hard life for a woman. I didn't expect this of America."

Rose scooped three spoonfuls of sugar into her brew. "This ain't hard. Hard hasn't started yet." She leaned farther across the table. "There's talk." Glancing around the room, her voice dropped lower still. "The women are organizing."

Kathleen was confused. "Organizing?"

"They're wanting to put a union in the factory. In all the factories. There's talk everywhere."

"I don't know what a union is," Kathleen admitted, keeping her voice quiet.

"It's where workers get together to improve the

conditions," Rose explained. "We want more money and shorter hours."

Kathleen closed her eyes. "What a wonderful idea. That must be what Bertha was talking about when she mentioned secret meetings."

"I know Bertha," Rose said, still whispering. "She's hot for a union. Others figure it'll only bring trouble. We'll lose our jobs."

"I can't afford to lose my job, Rose."

"You can't afford to work for these slave wages either."

"True enough."

"There's a meeting each week if you want to come. It's held in secret so the bloody bobbies don't come snooping around."

"Why would they come? Why would they be interested?"

"The bosses tell them to come and break up the meetings. They get mean sometimes. Last week one of the blokes put his big paw on a woman."

"No!"

"Shhh. She told him to go suck eggs, and he let go, but we decided we better be real private about the next get-together."

"How do you know who to tell there's a meeting?"

"We just kind of feel out the other person till we're sure of her. I'm telling you because I know you. I figure I can trust you whether you come along or not."

"You can trust me. But, Rose, I know a policeman, Patrick, and he's very nice. I don't know if all coppers are bad."

"Patrick," Rose said. "His mother's a factory girl. That's the only reason he's decent to us. A copper is a copper. Don't ever forget it."

Kathleen could not imagine Patrick harming her. "When's the next meeting?"

Rose moved from her seat and slid in next to Kathleen. "Tonight." She checked her watch. "Half an hour. Want to go?"

Kathleen was tired. But she was always tired. Morning, noon and night she was tired. She was never going to be rested. But did she want to get involved in something that might cost her her job? "I was hoping we might just sit and chat this evening. It's the first chance we've had."

Rose returned to her side of the booth. "That would be nice, but I want to go to the meeting." She was still whispering.

Kathleen added another teaspoon of sugar to her tea, disappointed that Rose would rather do something other than talk with her. Reluctantly, she agreed to go. She sipped from her cup, then carefully returned it to the saucer. "But if this looks like something I don't want to get involved in, sure I'll be leaving you and going home in a scat."

Rose smiled widely, displaying tea-stained teeth. "You won't be sorry. The women talk — complain, really, and somebody else writes notes. We're going to put together a paper about what we want, and someone's going to take it to the boss when it's done."

"You?"

"Never. I'm not that much of a fighter."

"You're the one who mentioned finding new fights on new soil," Kathleen reminded her.

"I did, didn't I? I believe we've got it, too."

They left Ellie's and strolled in the direction of the park. Along the way, the short, round red-headed Rebecca Swayze joined them. Kathleen knew who she was but had never talked with her. Rose introduced them.

"How do you like working on the machines?" Kathleen asked by way of conversation. Rebecca had only recently been moved to an electric machine.

"Better than sewing by hand," Rebecca answered.

She walked on the other side of Rose, rather closely to her, Kathleen thought. "I agree," she said. She could think of nothing else to say.

Rose chatted with Rebecca about other women in the factory, how they were feeling regarding tonight's meeting and how many they thought might show. Kathleen listened politely, feeling ignored. She supposed she should. She did not know what was going on regarding this union. She wondered why Bertha never brought it up with her again.

Located several blocks north from where they worked, just above Fourteenth Street, the park was an unlit affair. Two boys scurried into the bushes as they approached.

"They're watchers for us," Rose whispered. "Get twenty cents a night. They let us know if the bobbies are about." Rebecca nodded in confirmation.

Several women had already gathered a few yards away. "Thought you wasn't going to make it," someone said to Rebecca.

"Wouldn't miss it," Rebecca answered.

"Who's this?" another asked, approaching Kathleen.

Kathleen saw only shadowy faces. Not even a candle was lighted.

"Friend of mine," Rose murmured. "Kathleen O'Donald."

"Friend of that bloody copper, that's wot she is," came a thick brogue, followed by a cough and a hacking sound from her throat.

"You'd best send this one packing. She walks home with Officer Shawnery most every night." Kathleen recognized Bertha's voice.

A gravelly laugh ensued. "He walks with all the women, Bertha. Be glad he does or you'd probably have already lost your virginity to the rascals that hang about at night."

"Lost that forty years ago," Bertha quipped.

Snorts and coughs stifling laughter came from several quarters.

So that was why Bertha had stopped talking to her. Patrick! And she did not think it a bit funny that the women needed to have a policeman around or they would otherwise be attacked. "Probably go on forever," she told herself.

Rose stepped closer to her. "What'd you say, Kathleen?"

"I was talking to myself," Kathleen answered.

An unknown voice snapped, "Well, speak up, girlie. If you're gonna talk, talk so's the rest of us can hear."

The sassy voice made Kathleen's hackles rise. She moved purposefully to the center of the circle. "All right, I will." Her brogue thickened with her rising anger. "Don't ever call me girlie again. Don't call yourselves girlie. I don't like it, and I'll wager you don't. We have names. Let's use them."

"So you can report back to your copper friend?" Bertha challenged.

"No! So that I keep my identity. So that you keep yours. Make up a name if you want to, but don't let anyone take away who you are by calling you cheap names like 'girlie' and 'sweetheart' when you're nobody's sweetheart, and 'Kathy' when your name's Kathleen." Her voice rose. "We can do better than that as women and at least not steal ourselves from ourselves."

"Quiet!"

Kathleen recognized the voice and the tall, thin silhouette of Barbara Negley, a ninth floor worker from the Triangle. "You're right, Kathleen. We shouldn't cheapen ourselves and hereafter we won't." Her shadow turned to the group that had huddled, and then she faced Kathleen again. "But tonight the issue is not our identity, but our lives. Who's taking notes? Is Dot here?"

"Right here," came a small voice.

"Start writing then," Barbara said. "Let's discuss and then go home. I've got two kids waiting for me and I'm damn tired."

They spoke in broken Italian, German, Hungarian, English and Polish as they struggled to understand one another. A second language was developing that even Kathleen had learned to understand.

A single small candle was lighted for the

notetaker. The talk was tough, spoken by tough women. Low wages, the filth of the factories, long brutal hours, poor toilet room facilities and the lack of extra doors to leave the premises were mentioned. The women talked about the pain in their backs, legs, arms and hands from backless stools and fast machines. There was more, but numb with fatigue, Kathleen lost track as the list of concerns lengthened and the night wore on.

The meeting broke up at eleven-thirty, and Rose, Rebecca and she started home. Again Rose and Rebecca walked closely side by side while Kathleen felt much the tag-along. Rose and Rebecca were heavy into discussion until it was time for Rebecca to turn off.

Kathleen watched with some sense of jealousy as they hugged goodbye and wondered why she felt that way. Rose could have all the friends she wanted, and it seemed as if she had several, since a good number spoke with her after the meeting. If Kathleen continued coming, perhaps she could make more friends too, and not rely solely on Rose as her only friend. As long as Patrick continued walking her home so regularly, she would have to work hard at it.

It was another ten minutes before Rose stopped. "I turn off here."

"See you tomorrow," Kathleen said. She waited for Rose to hug her and she did. Kathleen's jealousy faded. She felt silly for having experienced it.

Releasing her, Rose asked, "Will you come to the next meeting with me?"

"I'll think about it, but yes, probably."

"I'd like that." Rose hugged her again, and each headed down her own street.

The lamp lighter had come and gone, the illumination barely adequate. Nervously hurrying home, Kathleen looked forward to the night when electric lights would be installed along Wooster Street.

CHAPTER EIGHT
Saturday, August 21, 1909

Kathleen woke with a start. Mr. Solinski was coughing badly, something he had done as long as Kathleen had known him. He seemed to be worse this morning, in fact, was worsening every morning. At breakfast she asked how long the Solinskis had been in America.

"Nine months," Sadie answered proudly. She took the time to dig around in a bureau drawer, returning with a photograph of the family minus the twins not yet born. In the background was the Statue of Liberty. In the heavy accent Kathleen had little trouble understanding anymore, she said, "We should not have spent the money on the photograph, but we wanted to show our grandchildren when we first came to America."

In the photo, Mr. Solinski was smiling, holding Sasha in his arms. Sadie stood closely by his side. Kathleen glanced in his direction. In nine months' time, he had become a skeleton of his former self. Kathleen had thought him to be in his late forties or early fifties. This picture suggested he was in his late twenties or early thirties. She smiled weakly and returned the picture to Sadie, who gazed lovingly at it before tucking it away.

Kathleen wondered if this was her future. She felt a cough welling up within her, fought it and lost. She hastened through breakfast, unable to bear the sound of Mr. Solinski's hacking, and was soon walking toward the factory.

It was no wonder he was sick, Kathleen thought, living in such nasty close quarters and working fourteen, sixteen, and sometimes twenty hours a day to meet his deadline. It was a miracle that the rest of the family was not sick as well.

Every Saturday the Solinskis' finished garments were picked up by the contractors and another consignment left behind. Kathleen thought there was even more brought during the week, but she did not ask and no one complained. It meant more money for the family.

At her table and depressed beyond endurance, Kathleen stared at her machine. The mechanical monster seemed to leer at her, seemed to grow larger. It looked as though it might swallow her. She felt a whisper of dread race through her and fought the sensation. After tucking her coat beneath her buttocks and placing her precious fifty-cent, wide-brimmed hat on the floor beside her lunch of cheese and bread, she waited for a floor boss to bring her today's work.

In no time, Howe cast a great heap of white cloth into her wicker basket. "Here's yer stint, girlie."

Seething, she bit her tongue. She hated the man, hated him so passionately that she wanted to ram her scissors deep into his hands that so carelessly threw down her work. She wanted to ram them through his tongue that so loosely and contemptuously spoke to her.

Nearby was a cuspidor, one of several throughout the shop and used none too accurately by the men. Howe spit and missed, his slime slithering slowly down the outside of the container.

Kathleen turned abruptly away. She thought she was going to be sick. She mustn't. She *mustn't*. Nearly panic-stricken, she looked around the room for something to focus on, something that was common to her everyday life — the hats and coats on the hooks in the cloakroom; the door to her eventual freedom twelve hours from now; Emily Wojnowski, an old woman seated next to her, who chatted incessantly from the side of her mouth to anyone who would listen. Nothing was working to bring back her concentration. *Nothing.* She was terrified. Her chest hurt, her heart pounding. Her hands and feet were going to sleep. She wanted to *run!*

She started to rise and felt a strong hand on her

shoulder. Like a cornered animal she turned to pull away from the awful, threatening grip.

"It's me, Kathleen. You're going to be all right. Just a bit of a hard morning you're having." Rose came into view. She kept her hand on Kathleen. "You'll be all right, dear. Here, eat this." Rose passed her a bright red apple. "It'll make you feel better."

Her eyes closed, Kathleen clutched the apple and breathed deeply, absorbing the warmth of Rose's hand, feeling it seep through her dress and skin and dip down into her chest, quelling her racing heart. The pain that gripped her like an iron band stopped.

She breathed deeply again and returned to her work without even wondering why Rose was out of her seat, away from her table, standing beside her. Even hearing Mr. Howe yell from across the room at Rose to get her ass back to her machine did not faze Kathleen. Numbly, she heard Rose curse under her breath and watched the brave woman return to her stool. Rose sat and slumped, as they all did here, picked up a piece of fabric and began sewing, but not before she looked across the room at Kathleen and smiled.

It was then that Kathleen felt herself calm down. She asked Emily, "Why is it that we cough so? It isn't just the lint."

The tiny, gray-haired woman said in broken Polish, another language Kathleen was becoming comfortable with, "It is the coughing sickness. I think in America it is called consumption. The women try to marry before they get it."

"But what causes it?"

"This place," Emily answered disgustedly. "It's filthy. No air, windows that don't open very well, doors that are locked, dirt and dust everywhere." She pointed a bony finger toward Inez Pankowski seated directly opposite them and whispered, "In a year, she'll be dead. Didn't marry soon enough. Listen to her. She's got it bad."

Kathleen grabbed the apple again and held it close to her. Her eyes became wild. She must not listen to this prattling old woman. She would live. *Live!* She would find a better way, a better life. This was America!

The moment passed, and she felt silly for having been so frightened, wondering what had triggered her irrational trepidation. But she had been more than just irrational. For the first time, she thought that she too might die from working in this factory. Throughout the morning, each time she coughed she thought about it. She thought about Mr. Solinski. Some high-minded woman would look quite lovely in what his hands had created while he sat in his dark little home with his too large family, sweating and coughing his life away and making more lovely clothing.

She ground her teeth as a fierce determination overcame her. She would do something about this hell on the eighth floor. She would never miss another union meeting.

That evening, she waited for Rose at the Greene Street entrance. Before Rose could voice her surprise at seeing her there, she grabbed Rose by the arm and dragged her to the side of the building. "I want to become a union supporter. I want to do it right now." She saw Patrick approaching them and plastered a smile across her face.

"Evening, ladies. Fine night." The night was unusually cold, but he always had a cheerful word to say.

"Sure and you're full of stardust, Patrick Shawnery," she said, willing herself to remain calm.

"Are you needing an escort this lovely evening?" He rocked back on shiny black shoes.

"Not this evening, kind sir."

"But we thank you just the same," added Rose.

He tipped his hat and wandered down the walk.

"I don't trust him," Rose said.

Kathleen looked after him. "I'll reserve judgment."

"There's a meeting tonight. We have time for coffee if you're caring to go."

"I'm caring to go," Kathleen assured her, "but sure I have no money for coffee."

"It'll be me treat. One full cup, two empty mugs."

When Kathleen and Rose arrived at the park, many others were already there. Bertha was heatedly reminding her listeners that a walkout was not anything new. There had been one in June the past year.

"That's right," spoke a clear voice. "That subcontractor stuck up for his girls. He was damn sick of the company slave-driving them."

Kathleen had learned very early that the women in the factories worked in groups run by individual subcontractors. These men worked for the company, which paid them directly, and they in turn paid the girls through the company. She had never seen her subcontractor and often wondered, as did all the women, how much he was paid. She only knew she never saw much money.

In the moonlight, the voice continued. "Dobbs laughed right out loud at him. And then the subcontractor threatened to take his girls with him, but he wasn't allowed to talk to any of them. He was fired, *fired* for sticking up for them."

"I remember," added another. "He figured they would slug him cold if they got him in the elevator, and so he asked somebody to go with him. And you girls . . ." She swung her hand in the general direction of the circle surrounding her. Kathleen watched the shadowy figure moving in an animated fashion. "You remember what happened. They grabbed him and dragged him out of the shop."

"Yeah, yeah," came an excited voice from behind Kathleen. "Must have been four hundred girls dropped their work and followed him, him screaming all the way, 'Will you stay at your machines and see a fellow worker treated this way?' I remember him yelling his head off like it was yesterday."

"And then what happened?" asked the original storyteller.

Barbara Negley said, "Everybody was back on the job in no time, so you can see how far that got us. We're all back here working again."

"Nobody wants to lose their jobs, Barbara," Inez Pankowski said. It surprised Kathleen that Inez, sick as she was, would be here.

"But if we'd stayed away, they would've given us raises."

"It ain't gonna happen," declared one. "Scabs move right in."

"We can bust their heads if they do."

"Oh, and that's the answer," said Bertha. "There's millions out there waiting for your job. You can't hit them all. We gotta get them to strike too. You want better pay, you're gonna have to fight like hell for it, and fight everybody else too."

From the outer fringes of the circle, Kathleen asked, "What about how dirty the place is?"

"Dirt? Who the hell cares about dirt? I care about money and hours. I don't give a shit about dirt." Bertha walked over to Kathleen. "You again."

"I'm here again, Bertha, and I'm here to stay," Kathleen retorted. "I'm concerned about money and hours too. Don't think I'm not. But I'm also concerned about the filth of the factory. It's probably like that in all the factories."

"I can't live on slave wages," said Acsy Jason. "I can live with dirt." She moved closer to Kathleen.

"No, you can't," Kathleen exclaimed. "Listen to yourselves. You're coughing. All of you. Listen!" She fought to stifle her brogue as she tore off her hat so that they could see her better. "You're in terrible trouble."

She knew she had spoken of an abiding fear. Fingers pierced by whirring needles could be sucked clean, but not the cough. Every single woman had already coughed at least once in the short time that Kathleen had been present at the meeting.

"Money's the point of the strike. We should keep things simple for the first demand." Salome Sumartono placed her hand firmly on Kathleen's arm. Her heavy body reeked of sweat and her short hair was shaggy and unkempt.

Angrily, Kathleen shook her off. "No! Go for more. Go for your lives." She stepped cautiously into

101

the middle of the gathering. "Today I was told of a woman who's going to die from the dust and dirt in a factory because she didn't marry and get out soon enough. I don't want to die because I didn't *marry* soon enough. And what about the men? If you women die, so do the men, and then you're widows working back in the factories again and breathing that filth again. Let's demand that they clean up the factory. It wouldn't take much to sweep the floor once a day and open the damn windows farther!" She'd be in confession again on Saturday, and she didn't give a damn! Damn, damn, *God*damn! Why not make it count?

"Well, I ain't sweeping no floor in no factory," came a voice from the back row. "I'm a seamstress, and a seamstress I'll stay."

Kathleen glowered at the unseen voice. "You think like that and you'll be dead in a year too, and if not a year, then soon. I don't know how soon, but you're dead. We all are. We'll die rich and rested. More money, less hours — and dead. Wonderful."

"All right, all right," Dot, the group's official notetaker, said. "She's got a point. What's it gonna cost us to add one more demand to our list? I'm kind of sick of kicking all that garbage away from my work area. Hell, the ninth floor ain't been swept in four, five weeks. And it smells of old rotten lunches. Phew! That bologna those women bring in, and garlic."

"You don't like garlic?"

"Shut up, you silly bunch of cackling hens!" someone said sharply. "Dot, make a note. We'll ask for clean floors —"

"And wide-opened windows!" somebody said.

"And toilet rooms. Add the toilets."

"You got all that?"

"I got it. We go in tomorrow with the list."

"Who's going?"

"Let's see." Dot brought the notes closer to the single candle held by Bertha. "We got Gisela, me, Bertha, Minna —"

"Jamison's girl?" Barbara stated in a choked voice. "She's practically management. She's probably going to marry him."

"He doesn't know a thing." Minna stood not five feet from Kathleen.

Warm, soft murmurs of support and encouragement quietly filled the air.

"Who else?" Bertha snapped.

"Myrtle Spilka," Dot concluded.

With the negotiators named, the rest split off and left the park. Rose took Kathleen's arm. "They'll discuss the list and plan how to face the bosses."

The very thought of standing before Dobbs scared Kathleen. And it would not be just him. Both owners of the Triangle, Mr. Blanck and Mr. Harris, would be there too. She dropped her head and prayed she would not be fired, would not get sick, would not starve to death in the great land of America.

"Hey, honey, why look so gloomy? Don't worry. The girls who are going to do it were carefully chosen. They agreed. They can face those so-and-so's. We'll get what we want."

Kathleen began perspiring. She never realized how protected she had been all her life until she had come to the United States. She had lived alone after her parents died, but there had been her familiar home to comfort her, friends dating back to school days, kind men who courted her. Here there was only Rose who lived many blocks away down unfamiliar streets. She removed her hat and leaned heavily against Rose.

"It'll be all right, honey."

Kathleen liked being called honey. Her mother used to call her that. She did not feel like she had lost her identity because Rose seemed to mean it when she used the endearing term. "You sound like my ma," she said.

Rose smiled, giving Kathleen's arm a friendly squeeze. "I'm too young. I could be an older sister."

"Yes, that would work," Kathleen said. "I have no sister, nor brother, nor parents."

Rose put her arm around Kathleen's shoulders, drawing her close. "You have me, Kathleen." She dropped her arm, and they walked silently toward Bleecker Street. "You want me to walk you home?" she asked.

Kathleen looked up at her, the street lamp glinting weakly off her eyes. "No, I'll be fine."

They hugged goodbye. It was a longer hug than usual and when they broke apart, both giggled.

"That was nice," Rose said.

"We could do it again," Kathleen suggested.

They did, and Kathleen suddenly felt awkward and silly, listening to Rose giggle again.

Shyly, Kathleen looked down at her shoes wearing thin around the toes where daily she hooked her feet into the stool's rung to keep her steady. "I'll see you tomorrow."

Rose lifted Kathleen's chin with her hand. "Yes."

Kathleen had trouble looking into Rose's eyes partially concealed in the shadow of her hat brim.

Rose held Kathleen's face for a long time with just a knuckle. Kathleen wondered what was going through the Englishwoman's mind. It must be a pleasant thing, Kathleen thought, for she felt good things coming from her.

Rose dropped her hand. "Tomorrow."

Kathleen nodded. She waited for Rose to say something else, but she remained silent and statue-like.

Kathleen walked away, now and then glancing back until she rounded the corner, Rose still looking after her.

Kathleen felt marvelous, the best she had since the day she had decided in Ireland to come to America.

CHAPTER NINE

Sunday, October 3, 1909

The leaves on the few trees that lined Wooster Street had turned varying shades of orange, brown, red and yellow. Skies were clear, the October air brisk with a pleasant tang. For once, the odors of factory smoke that continuously filled the city were faint. More prominent was the smell from coal fires burning, heating buildings.

Kathleen breathed deeply of the rich autumn air and immediately began coughing. Lately, it had become a frequent occurrence, enough so that she had walked by other factories in the area to see if they might be cleaner than the Triangle. She gave up hope when she saw how identical they all were: tall, sooty buildings that took more than they would ever give. Give, she had scoffed. Those places gave nothing!

By the time she had crossed under the Sixth Avenue El and reached St. Joseph's doors, she was in turmoil, resentful and bitter that her American dreams were disintegrating like so much factory dust.

She attended high mass especially for the opportunity to stay away longer from the stifling atmosphere of the Solinskis' apartment. She was becoming more and more nervous as Mr. Solinski's health degenerated. That morning Sadie had had to help him out of bed and to his machine.

At home again, she noticed an immediate difference within the apartment before entering. She could hear none of the usual sounds — no treadle machine clacking away, no chattering among the family. As tired as they were, they often talked among themselves.

Confused, she opened the door just as Joe Grashow, the neighbor who had hollered at her that first night back from work, stuck his head out and said, "They carried him off, miss, right after you went out. He was blue as a bairn's eyes, he was, trying to breathe, his wife clinging and screaming all the way, and the daughter, too, and the other two being carried along. It was a bloody mess, I tell you. He's dead, he is, sure as I'm standing here. Coughed himself right into the grave."

He sounded joyous, delivering such terrible news. "Sure, and you're mistaken, sir," Kathleen said, glancing at him and then at the empty apartment. "There wasn't that much the matter with Mr. Solinski. Perhaps he was taken to the hospital."

"Hospital, is it?" Grashow scratched his belly. "And just where from the King's court do you come from?" Laughing, he closed his door. Through thin walls, Kathleen heard him say to his overbearing and obnoxious wife, "High-stepping lady, that one. She'll get hers one day, her head in the cloud, it is."

Kathleen closed the apartment door on the woman's cackling laughter and walked to the center of the room, feeling its gloom weigh her down. Everything was still there — the sewing machine, needles handily stuck into the wallpaper over to the left, spools of thread piled high in a basket on the floor to her right, the table stacked with work that had been going on since breakfast, pieces of garments covering the floor, chairs and beds. Everything was here except the Solinskis.

"Lord, and this is an awful mess." She drew in a shuddering breath. "What do I do now?"

Her answer knocked on the door, and Grace rolled in unannounced. "We gotta talk, Kathy, darling."

Kathleen bristled at Grace's familiarity, barely managing to speak pleasantly. "Please come in."

Without preamble, her landlady said, "You're alone now. I'll be expecting you to take over the rent or move out, or in with somebody else. Take in another family or a girl or two, but I gotta get full rent or put you out. That's the way it is." She put her hands on her hips. "I'm a businesswoman first and last."

"I'll see to it," Kathleen said, at once dismayed as to how to go about finding others willing to help pay for this wretched flat.

"I'll be putting a sign in the window. You'll fill the place in no time."

"What's the rent?" Kathleen asked.

"Fifteen a month," Grace announced and was gone.

Kathleen sank to a chair. Fifteen dollars a month. That was more than a month's salary.

There was no time to dwell upon this catastrophic news before a second knock sounded.

"What *is* it?" She yanked off her hat and slung it aside. Impatiently, she ran her hands through her hair. Hairpins scattered to the floor. Her long hair fell in waves around her shoulders. She shoved it behind her ears and answered the door.

Two heavily moustached men stood with several cloth bags in their hands. "We come to get the work." They both stepped forward as if to pass her.

She remained unmoving. "What work, Edgar?" she asked the familiar contractor, recognizing him as the man who, each Saturday, delivered garment pieces to the family.

"The Solinskis worked for me. And this here stuff is mine. Yarrow here'll help me take it out." A skinny, sallow man accompanied Edgar.

"Nothing moves," Kathleen said. She did not trust a living soul right now. "For all I know, you're the man in the moon and believing you can light a penny-candle from it."

"Go get Grace," he said. "She'll vouch for me."

Kathleen debated whether or not she should. After all, the Solinskis were not her family. She had only slept here, eaten with them, taken care of the children, occasionally rocked the twins to sleep, helped nurse one of them who had taken sick back to health. By the time these memories had piled up, she felt a kinship to the Solinskis she had never felt before. What if they returned and their work was gone and she had been here and done nothing to stop the removal of the garments, the very ones that put food on the table and kept a roof over their heads, hers included.

"Wait here," she said. She locked the door and brushed by them.

"You'll see, girlie," Edgar said to her back.

She paused, debating whether or not to tell him to address her properly. No, she decided. One way or the other, he and Yarrow would be gone in moments. It was not worth her time.

She returned shortly, Grace panting up the stairs behind her. "Well, hello, Edgar. You picking up the work?"

"Got to. They ain't gonna be back."

"Give it to Kathy, here. She never misses work. I see her going out every day. She'd be steady."

"How about it, girlie? You want the work? Got a machine already and plenty to do." Edgar hovered over her, inching closer to her as he spoke.

Something went *ping* in her head. Her eyes became unfocused as sweat popped out on her forehead. Her body trembled, and she screamed, "Don't you ever call me girlie again, you overgrown garlic clove. I wouldn't do your work for you if I was starving. You have killed a good man by overworking him, and who knows what'll happen to his family? Get out! Get out, and take your bloody rags with you. And take your Goddamn *machine* with you too."

Her brogue became thick as bread dough as she advanced upon Edgar.

Doors up and down the hallway were opening as Grace unlocked Kathleen's door. Edgar edged into the apartment as she continued her tirade of rage while marching directly at him.

Yarrow rapidly and unceremoniously began stuffing bags, unmindful of neatness, only wanting to get the job done and get out. "Come on, Ed. Move yer arse." Another bag stuffed, he slung it into the hallway.

Edgar had now been backed to the farthest wall. "What's she saying, Grace? What's she bawling about?" He held up his hands in front of his lanky frame to ward off possible slaps.

Grace's large belly rolled with laughter. "I believe you're being told to pack and git, and if I was you, I'd be quick about it."

"Bitch!" he bellowed at Kathleen as he sidled past the raving woman. He grabbed the final sack, stuffing it full as Yarrow snatched up the treadle machine, grunting under its weight, and hurriedly dragged it out. Grace, still guffawing wildly, followed them. She gave Kathleen a big wink and pulled the door behind her.

Trembling, Kathleen closed her eyes and breathed deeply, attempting to let go of useless anger. She leaned against the door, surveying the place. It was empty, lifeless, her footsteps hollow against the wooden floor. Not three hours ago an entire family

111

had lived here: a husband, a wife, their children. And now — not even the basket of spools of thread.

She walked over to the bureau and pulled open the top drawer. Inside were a few pieces of clothing and the photograph album. She drew out the book, sat at the barren table and slowly flipped through the pages. There were not many pictures, a few taken apparently in Poland and a few from America. The one of the Solinskis that Sadie had shown her was the final photograph. Kathleen's eyes teared as she studied the family, their eyes alive with hope, great smiles stretching across their faces as they stood before the Lady. Would anyone come to claim the clothes and the album? Did anyone care what became of the Solinskis? She was sure they had been unable to save a penny against a day such as this. She put her head down on the album and cried.

She had not been weeping a minute before there came another knock. She growled deep in her throat, animal-like, ready to attack. Grace could wait a day for the rent. She swung it wide to tell her just that.

"Hello, Kathleen."

It was paralyzing to see Rose there, a smile on her face which rapidly faded as tears gushed from Kathleen's eyes, flowing in rivulets down her cheeks.

"What is it, love?"

Kathleen fell against Rose, burying her face against her chest. Kathleen felt so small, so insecure. As if she were a child, Rose took her in her arms and gently steered her into the room kicking the door shut behind her.

Dusky light fell upon them. Rose's arms were like steel bands around her. Kathleen trembled uncontrollably, sobs wracking her body, fingers clutching the lapels of Rose's coat, digging in until they ached.

She jerked Rose closer to her, sobbing, "It's not fair, it's not fair, it's not fair."

"What's not fair, love?" She rested her cheek against the top of Kathleen's head.

"Mr. Solinski died. In less time than it takes me to walk to church, his entire family was gone from here, their work taken away. Nothing is left but bits of clothing and some photographs. That's all. Nothing else at all. What a waste." She was nearing hysteria.

Rose stopped her two or three times asking her to repeat something, so incoherent had she become. "Here, darling, you're beginning to frighten me. Come, sit down."

"I don't want to sit. I sit all the *time.*" She coughed violently. "I think I'm going to be sick."

"You're upset, Kathleen. Lie down a while. Come on now, that's a good girl."

Still feeling like a child, and knowing she sounded a good deal like one, she allowed Rose to lead her to the bed. "It's always buried during the day, but now . . ." She began to sob.

"Come on, love. Here, lie beside me." Rose lay down and drew Kathleen into her arms. Kathleen pulled a handkerchief from the cuff of her sleeve. She dried her eyes and blew her nose before settling against Rose. She remembered sobbing a while longer and the feel of secure arms around her before she fell asleep.

It was dark when she woke. Rose was sitting at the kitchen table, the chimney lamp burning low. She had shed her coat, revealing a brown dress that

Kathleen always thought looked nice on her. Kathleen rose and stretched.

Rose smiled. "You're awake."

"I slept hard. I never sleep during the day."

"How could you, with work piled all over your bed and you at work yourself?"

Kathleen studied her closely, feeling her heart stir. "You're very beautiful, Rose."

"Now, aren't we the one to be full of blarney?"

Kathleen smiled. "It's true. You can't deny it."

"I don't see it in meself."

Kathleen came to the table and sat kittycorner to Rose. She reached up and pushed aside a strand of hair that had fallen across Rose's forehead. Her fingers trailed down the side of Rose's temple and followed a path of shadow to her mouth.

Rose turned so that her lips touched Kathleen's finger. Kathleen let out a long, soft sigh. She had been in a terrible rage but a few hours ago. Now, she felt peaceful. Rose had the capacity to put her to rest when Kathleen was feeling just awful. She wondered how Rose could do that to her.

"I feel safe when I'm with you, Kathleen," Rose whispered against her fingertips.

Her lips were soft, the softest thing Kathleen had ever known. She closed her eyes as Rose turned her head just enough to allow her mouth to rest in the palm of Kathleen's hand. Her breath was warm against her skin. "You're a good friend, Rose, to spend your afternoon with me. I'm sure you must have things to do. Mending, washing your clothes, perhaps a letter you wanted to write."

114

Rose shifted and tipped her head so that her forehead was cupped in Kathleen's palm. She rocked her face slightly from side to side. With her own hand she pressed Kathleen's more firmly against her forehead. "There is nothing that cannot keep if you need me here."

Kathleen moved her hand to the back of Rose's neck and tenderly squeezed it. She pulled Rose toward her a bit.

Rose slid from her chair, kneeling before Kathleen, laying her head against Kathleen's breast. Rose's eyes were closed, and with her thumb, Kathleen stroked the long lashes resting like silken strands against Rose's cheek.

"I feel such lovely warmth from your hand, Kathleen. It soothes me. A shameful thing when I should be soothing you."

"You do soothe me, Rose Stewart. I slept soundly in your arms. I woke rested. I don't remember being so rested in a long time."

Rose smiled. "I said it before, and I'll say it again. You Irishmen are full of blarney. The whole bloody lot of you."

"Sure, and that's the truth."

Their laughter died away and as though rehearsed, both stood, putting their hands on each other's waists.

Kathleen felt herself being drawn into Rose's eyes, felt herself falling without moving, saw the gray of Rose's eyes surround, then engulf her. Slowly, Rose bent her head to Kathleen's, stopping just before the tips of their noses touched.

"You're a lovely lass," Rose whispered.

"And I've already said that you are, Rose Stewart, so don't be fishing for compliments, for you'll not receive them from me."

Rose displayed a sweet smile. Only a breath separated them. "Darling," she whispered and pressed her lips against Kathleen's.

Kathleen felt Rose's pliant mouth against her own and closed her eyes. A great sphere of air filled her lungs. Rose's strong arms wrapped around her and pulled her close, her hand cradling Kathleen's head.

Rose released her, burying her face in the hollow of Kathleen's shoulder.

Blushing, Kathleen tried to step back, but Rose held her tightly. Kathleen became aware of Rose's large breasts pressing against her. The kiss had been so powerful that she had not noticed before. Now she was conscious of each one, large celestial bodies of exquisite flesh.

Rose's hips pressed against her. A hard bone hit Kathleen just above her own very private place. Rose moved slightly, side to side, thrusting against her. She was taking Kathleen's breath away.

Kathleen wondered if she too should move as Rose was doing. It felt so good. Rose was a close, close friend. Kathleen thrust her hips slightly against her to see what would happen, to see if Rose would be able to feel her like she was feeling Rose.

Rose let out a gasp and then another, frightening Kathleen.

"Are you all right?" Kathleen asked. She frowned

and tipped Rose's head up. "Look at me. Are you all right?"

Rose's eyes were closed. "I'm all right. You just are so beautiful that you take me breath away."

"Don't talk foolish, Rose. No one is that beautiful."

"You are, Kathleen, you are. 'Tis a wonder that you've not married, that men aren't throwing themselves at your feet, paving the way everywhere you walk."

Kathleen stepped back. "You're a silly woman."

Rose moved close to Kathleen again. She did not touch her, but rather gazed into her eyes. "I would be the first to fall before you, Kathleen O'Donald."

Kathleen stared in bewilderment. "You're a strange one, Rose. Strange, indeed."

"Strange, how?"

Kathleen shrugged in confusion. "You kissed me, made me want to kiss you. I haven't been kissed in such a fashion by a woman."

"Never?"

"Never. When I was a little girl, another little girl and I played house a time or two, and I kissed her, but it wasn't the same. I haven't thought of the incident in years."

"Romantic friendships aren't strange," Rose said. "I've been in a few and they're not strange." Her voice was low, breathy, heavy. She spoke against Kathleen's ear. "In romantic friendships, the women kiss each other like we just did."

"Do they now?" Kathleen's heart thudded. She could feel the rapid, steady beat of Rose's heart too.

"Aye, they do." Again, Rose's face was only a fraction of an inch from Kathleen's.

"And do these women have many such friendships?" Kathleen asked.

"Some do. Some don't."

"Why ... why ..." It was becoming increasingly difficult for Kathleen to think. "Why," she tried again, "would some have more than others?"

"Some women," Rose whispered in Kathleen's ear, "find a woman who suits them for life, and they remain together until death. Others are more the roving kind and find many such friendships."

"Where are these women?"

"In England, here ... everywhere, I guess."

"I've never met them."

"Difficult to find unless you yourself are such a woman."

"You, yourself?"

"I'm such a woman."

"Are you the roving kind?" Kathleen asked, a bit disappointed that Rose had kissed other women.

"Only because I've not found a woman I would live with for life."

Kathleen pulled back. "I can't imagine it. What about the husbands? Don't they wonder about their wives kissing a woman? Especially the way you just kissed me. It seems almost sinful."

"There usually aren't husbands, and why sinful?"

"Well ... well." Kathleen searched for words. "I don't know. It just seems that ..." Silence hung thick in the room, and then she asked, "Why aren't there husbands?"

"We don't need them."

"Not need them? Not need a husband? Every woman needs a husband."

"Not all."

"I don't believe it."

"Not all."

Rose bent to kiss her again. Kathleen remembered the fire in her legs that raced up her thighs as her lips met Rose's. The fire was there again, and she pressed against Rose.

Rose drew her even tighter than she had during the first kiss. "Let me stay the night."

Kathleen's head was swimming. "You could. There's an extra bed now."

"I was thinking of sleeping in your bed . . . with you."

Kathleen's knees turned to water.

"I'd like to hold you all night long." Rose spoke softly.

She looked into Kathleen's eyes. Kathleen's eyes closed as she mumbled affirmatively, "Of course, that would be nice."

Rose stepped back leaving Kathleen standing unsteadily. "We need to be thinking of practical things," she said.

Kathleen eyes snapped opened. "Practical things?"

"We must eat."

Still stationary, Kathleen asked, "Are we having a romantic friendship?"

"We are in the beginnings of one, I would say." Rose put a hand on Kathleen's shoulders. "There is much more to such a friendship than you know."

"Will I be one of many?" Kathleen asked. Pangs of jealousy filled her mind.

"It's never me intention to find a new romantic friendship. I'd always hoped that each one I'd become involved in was the one that would last. I suspect this one is the one that will."

"Why would this one last and not one of the others?" Kathleen moved to the table and sat down.

Rose joined her. "As you learn more about what such a friendship is, I'll explain. Right now we need to think about eating and how you might continue to live here, or you could move in with me. There are three other girls there, and the room is much smaller, but it's possible. You could think about it."

"I will."

"And while we fix supper, think about how I'll be holding you all night long."

Kathleen did. She also thought about how all night long she would like to do a little of the holding herself.

CHAPTER TEN
Sunday, October 3, 1909

Kathleen stepped out to use the bathroom. Latching the hook behind her she leaned against the door, her eyes closed, her heart racing. Rose's kiss! The intensity of it! Kathleen had been kissed by men before, remembering they had left her longing for something else. But until Rose had kissed her she had never fully appreciated the power a kiss could hold, the charge it could send throughout her being, shooting from the ends of her fingers, through each strand of hair and out the tips of her toes.

A sharp knock on the door sent vibrations through the wood and into her spine. She stifled a shriek and moved to the sink. "I'm hurrying," she called.

She quickly splashed her face and with a washcloth, she reached beneath her blouse and cleansed her underarms. She smelled like a working girl. The odor of sweat that permeated the factory was in all her clothing. Washing clothes in the sink took valuable time and precious energy. Refreshing powder cost money, and a bath more than twice a week took too much effort.

In her absence, Rose had moved a chair to the side of the double bed. On the chair was the lantern burning low.

But stunning Kathleen into immobility was Rose herself. Near the single pillow they would share sat Rose. She had disrobed to midwaist, her dress dropped to her hips. Her hair was draped on either side of her shoulders, covering her breasts. The low light cast seductive shadows, softening the lines in her face. She reached up and slowly caressed a lock of her hair, her hand then coming to rest in her lap.

Kathleen's intake of breath was audible, Rose's beauty striking her like a powerful, physical blow. She was unable to move. Somehow she managed to lock the door. She stopped a few feet from Rose to behold her.

Rose's eyes softened, each dotted with a single highlight cast by the lantern's light. Her long lashes glistened as she blinked. Again, she touched her hair as if to be sure it was still in place, her fingertips stopping to caress her own breast.

Kathleen felt her nipples harden against the fabric of her blouse. She was rooted to the floor, her head swimming. She was unable to close the gap between herself and this woman much too beautiful to sleep beside, too beautiful to touch. Visions of clean, white clouds emptied her mind of the day's disasters. In awesome wonder, she was capable only of slowly shaking her head from side to side at the radiant vision before her.

She extended a hand, but Rose did not offer hers in return. Kathleen remain poised, her arm, hand and fingers extended.

An eternity later, Kathleen took another step forward and then another until she was finally within reach of Rose. Her breath panting heavily through flaring nostrils, her lips slightly parted, Kathleen slipped her hands beneath Rose's hair and placed them on Rose's shoulders. Rose tipped her head back and closed her eyes. Her skin was smooth as silk, the muscles beneath, strong as an oaken stave.

Kathleen could feel Rose's bones through her flesh. This was a woman; these were a woman's contours put together by the Lord God Almighty. What a beautiful job He had done. How had He known to create such a being? Kathleen lowered her head and opened her eyes, releasing a long breath.

Rose was intently studying her. "I fall into your eyes," she whispered. "You walk through me."

Wondrously, Kathleen looked at her. She wanted to move her hands, and she could not. Rose was too sacred to be handled by anyone, anyone at all. And yet somewhere, someone had. Rose had said so.

Kathleen felt explosive jealousy tear through her. For Rose to have been touched by others . . . She was too beautiful, too precious.

Kathleen closed her eyes again and knelt before Rose. She felt comfortable on her knees. Intoxicated.

She slid her hands down Rose's arms, to the crook of her elbows, down her forearms and hands. She studied Rose's hands, observing the calloused palms, the long slender fingers, the scratches on her knuckles.

Rose bent over her, placing her face against Kathleen's hair. They remained like that for several moments, their breathing unsteady, shallow and sometimes deep.

Kathleen came to her feet and withdrew not an inch before Rose grabbed her, placing her hands back on Rose's shoulders. The obvious desire in Rose's eyes, her wish to have Kathleen's hands touch her nearly buckled Kathleen's knees.

"I have never seen anyone or anything as beautiful as you, Rose. Never, never, never."

"To be sure, lass, there never was such as you, either."

Rose sounded distant, as if speaking from a long way off. Kathleen flexed her fingers only slightly to be sure that Rose was real and that, indeed, she was not dreaming.

Rose turned her head and rested a cheek against Kathleen's hand. Kathleen caressed Rose's hair starting at the part in the middle of her scalp, down the blond mane, feeling her ears and slender throat. She continued her movement the length of Rose's hair, moving her hands over her chest, then over her breasts still hidden by Rose's thick hair, to her lap and to what lay there.

Her eyes remained closed as she continued touching Rose. She felt Rose's hands cover hers, warm and moist. Rose rested her hands on the backs of Kathleen's, riding them over her shoulders. Again, Kathleen's knees turned to jelly. Rose guided their hands to her chest, then pushed them lower.

Kathleen knelt again, and as she did, Rose whispered her name. Of their own volition, her hands moved as if in a dream to Rose's breasts.

Someone made a sound; Kathleen was not sure who. She felt the rise and fall of Rose's chest, felt the swell of Rose's breasts as she breathed. Rose's nipples hardened like tiny stones, and where her breasts curved downward, Kathleen pressed against her chest and touched her ribs.

All of this — all of the gazing, the inability to believe that she could or should touch Rose, and then finally touching her — was more than Kathleen could comprehend. Without a thought in her head, with total disregard over the why or wonder of it, she pushed Rose backward on the bed and fell on her, wrapping her arms around her neck and shoulders, pressing herself against Rose, feeling Rose's mound against her own. The softness of Rose's breasts, which she had not yet seen but only felt, made Kathleen faintheaded. She pressed her cheek hard against Rose's, their shared breathing louder in Kathleen's ears than the rush of the elevated trains roaring by on Sixth Avenue.

She slid her mouth toward Rose's, felt the skin bunch up and smooth out as their cheeks pressed together. At last, their lips molded together. Kathleen pushed hard, smearing Rose's lips with her own. Kathleen kissed her cheeks, eyes, nose, chin, throat, trying to fuse with Rose, trying to get closer. She buried her face deep in Rose's hair.

Rose removed the rest of her clothing, Kathleen never once letting go of her, helping Rose out of the tangle of cloth and leather, buttons and snaps. Finally she was freed, and Kathleen positioned herself between Rose's legs, forcing them apart, thrusting herself against Rose, listening to Rose's soft moans.

Tears ran down Kathleen's cheeks and onto Rose's face. Rose brushed them away. "Why do you cry, love?"

"I can't get close enough to you."

"Then remove your clothes."

Rose's words sent pleasurable pain rocketing through Kathleen's chest. She tore off her clothing and within minutes was back on the bed and lying beside Rose. Again the thought that Rose was too beautiful to touch swept over her.

Rose laid a hand against Kathleen's cheek. "Completely perfect in every way." Kathleen felt her body break out in perspiration everywhere Rose's gaze fell upon her. "Except that you're way too thin."

"You're thin too but oh, so very, very beautiful." Kathleen's hand hovered above Rose's cheek, her shoulder, her hip.

"Why do you hesitate, Kathleen? Why do you not touch me?"

"Should the loveliest flower in all of England be disturbed?"

"I am to be disturbed, but only by you, Kathleen O'Donald. Only by you."

Kathleen felt slightly let down. "You say that in all your romantic friendships."

" 'Tis true, but I hope each will be me last. Perhaps you'll stay by me."

"And who could not?" Kathleen asked.

Rose raised up on one elbow. She slid her hand beneath Kathleen's neck, tangling her fingers in her hair. "Your hair is beautiful, love."

Kathleen sighed deeply. Rose called her "love." She remained with eyes closed as Rose kissed her throat, her breastbone, her belly. Rose's hands slid around her bellybutton and over her jutting hipbone. Her nails raked the insides of Kathleen's thighs and knees, making Kathleen involuntarily draw up her knees and move them apart.

She felt something warm trickle out of her private place and experienced a flash of fear that her time had started. Quick calculation told her she was far from that moment. This was something else, and she remembered the female farm animals when they were ready for breeding, what they looked like, how they reacted to the bulls and stallions.

She drew her knees together and lowered them. "Stop."

Rose paused. "What is it?"

"I'm not a farm animal."

Perplexed, Rose said, "I never suggested you were. Why would you even think that, especially now?"

"Who knows?" Kathleen lied. "I just don't want to be treated like one, or to behave like one."

127

"Never would I treat you like an animal, and you certainly aren't behaving like one. You're behaving like a woman who would like very much to be loved."

"I am?"

"Yes, you are," Rose whispered against her ear. "If you're uncomfortable, we'll stop. Never will I have you thinking you're being used as an animal or for that matter, being used at all. I'm sorry you think that or that I made you believe it."

"You didn't. It's just that I don't know what's happening to me."

"Everything natural is happening to you as it is to me. Let me show you, love. Give me your hand. You're doing all that you're supposed to be doing, to yourself and to me."

She guided Kathleen's hand to each of their breasts. "See? We're hard. It's because we long to be touched by fingers and mouths." Kathleen again felt a wetness over which she had no control. "And feel here," Rose was saying as she moved her hand to Kathleen's own mound. "See how wet you are, how ready." Kathleen barely felt her own wetness when she quickly snatched away her hand. "It's not right."

"Of course it's right," Rose assured her. "It's happening to me too. Feel me."

Reluctantly, Kathleen allowed Rose to guide her there. It was overpowering. Rose overflowed as Kathleen was doing. "You're wetting the bed."

"I'm not, love, and neither are you. This is love for each other. That's all it is. See how warm we are, each of us. This is how we're supposed to be. Haven't you ever once touched yourself? Been curious about why you feel so good there sometimes? In fact, made yourself feel good?"

"No," Kathleen said timidly. Her voice dropped to a whisper. "When we were seven, the priest in the confessional warned the girls. The nuns told us bad things would happen if we were touched before marriage."

Rose groaned and fell back onto the pillow. Shaking her head in despair, she said firmly, "Christ, seven years old. Kathleen, nothing bad is going to happen to you. Nothing at all. Something very wonderful is going to happen to both of us. You'll think you died and went to heaven. I know I'll think that because I know how beautiful touching you and you touching me is going to be."

"You would know, wouldn't you?"

"I'm older."

"Yes," Kathleen said. "And you say, I'm normal."

"As normal as rain, love. As normal as rain."

Kathleen forgot the animals on her Ireland farm and pulled Rose to her.

This time Rose laid herself on Kathleen who spread her legs. Rose slipped between them moving rhythmically against Kathleen.

"I'm so wet, though," Kathleen said.

"You're so ready," Rose replied. She reached between Kathleen's legs positioning her hand against her mound.

Kathleen gritted her teeth in pleasure and felt Rose slide a finger between Kathleen's lips. "You're swollen, girl."

"Is it natural?"

"All of what you are going through is natural,

darling. Don't let any man or woman in a black and white suit tell you different."

Kathleen forgot about the men and women in black and white suits at home and here, and enjoyed Rose moving her finger up and down on Kathleen's hot flesh. She gasped when it became too intense. Rose stopped for a second or two, then began again.

Their bodies still compressed, Kathleen experienced white heat building somewhere within her. She tried to identify its source. Was it Rose's finger moving maddenly up and down Kathleen's wetness with soft strokes and steady rhythm? No, it came from somewhere behind her, yet within her. Her back maybe; no, lower still; her thighs.

Then the climax hit her. She strained against Rose's hand which played lightly upon her as her hips arched higher and higher.

She felt a rough palm across her mouth, and she fought the hand smothering her and the one within her. She lost both battles until the fierce wonderful feelings rampant in her groin peaked. Then her mouth was freed and the hand removed from within her.

"You were screaming," Rose said softly. "You sounded like you were being murdered."

Kathleen lay limp beneath her. "I heard no screaming."

"You were screaming," Rose assured her, running a finger lightly across her mouth. "Loudly."

Kathleen did not argue. Rose was wrong. She never heard a sound.

Rose moved off to lie by Kathleen's side and take her in her arms. "You're so small. I love holding you. I love being able to hold so much of you all at once. This is very unlike a man who always does the holding, the woman always being the small one."

"But I'm a woman."

"So am I," said Rose, "and that's the joy of it."

"You are senseless."

"And so are you."

"You make me so," Kathleen murmured, moving against Rose. There were Rose's breasts, large and warm, the nipple not an inch from Kathleen's lips. Dare she suckle it? Oh, how she longed to take it within her mouth, to lie in Rose's arms and just suck on her forever.

She felt Rose's hand on the back of her head, felt her lips press against the top of Kathleen's head. Rose pulled Kathleen's face forward and to her breast. Kathleen parted her lips and took Rose's nipple in her mouth. It was as firm as set cheese, warm as a stone in the sun, tender as a newborn babe.

Kathleen's chin and nose were buried in the soft flesh surrounding the brown skin circling Rose's nipple. Kathleen moaned with great pleasure and contentment, surprised to find her hand on the coarse hair between Rose's legs. She did not recall how it happened to be there. Every move she made seemed so sensibly natural that she had only to exist and everything else simply fell into place.

She became wild with passion, listening to Rose's breathing steadily increase, listening to her voice say over and over, "Kathleen, love, I could never leave you, never." Rose clamped herself against Kathleen, wrapping a long leg over and around Kathleen's own, locking Kathleen to her.

Kathleen moved from Rose's nipple, her tongue

licking at Rose's skin as she moved toward her throat where she kissed her repeatedly. "Why do you make me feel this way, Rose, darling? Why do you make it seem so right?"

"It is, me dear, it is right." Rose began to rise over Kathleen, but Kathleen pushed her down and instead, lay on Rose and parted her legs. For the first time, flesh to flesh, hair to hair, thigh to thigh, belly to belly, breast to breast, Kathleen experienced another human being's full reaction to her. Slowly, they rocked together, Kathleen, low enough on Rose's chest to kiss Rose's breasts. Rose burrowed her face in Kathleen's hair, taking it by the handfuls and rubbing it across her face and moaning lowly, softly, continuously.

Knowing only what Rose had shown her, Kathleen placed a hand between Rose's legs, her fingers moving inside Rose. It was a deep place full of ridges and folds and wet heat.

She had barely begun to move her fingers, when Rose grasped Kathleen to her in a bone-crunching grip, bending her head to bite Kathleen's shoulder. Kathleen stifled a cry and stopped moving.

"Ah, God," Rose whispered fiercely. "Dear, dear lady, what have you done to me?"

Kathleen quickly withdrew her hand and began to move away, afraid she had hurt Rose. "I'm sorry, I'm . . ."

"You have filled me . heart," Rose whispered against her, her grip hard and solid on Kathleen. "You have filled me heart. I wish I could swallow you."

Kathleen knew then that what had hit her earlier had just hit Rose. "Sure, and that would be a grand thing, Rose, darling, a grand thing indeed. I would like to be swallowed by you and swallow you as well."

They lay side by side, silent, their breathing steadying. They admired the shadows changing on their bodies as they made slight adjustments for better comfort.

"What would the good nuns and priests think, now?" Rose asked, half laughing.

Yes, wondered Kathleen, what would they?

CHAPTER ELEVEN
Monday, October 4, 1909

Rose glanced up from her machine as Kathleen entered the factory. Her smile deeply warmed Kathleen as she grinned from an overflowing of well-being. Rose winked rakishly at her. Kathleen dropped her eyes, her face burning.

Rose had left late the previous night. Kathleen pleaded with her to stay, but she had refused. It was easier, she said, to leave for work from her own apartment.

Kathleen had been uneasy about Rose's going. For the first time since coming to the United States, Kathleen was alone. She was acutely aware of the apartment's night sounds, so very different from when the Solinskis had been there. There was no coughing, no children breathing peacefully just beyond the blanket that concealed her from the others, no creaking of the bed as the adults restlessly tossed and turned.

Sweating with worry, she had lain awake until dawn listening to the flat's quietness, wondering if Rose had made it home safely. What an insane thing to do — walk the streets unescorted at two in the morning.

During their lovemaking, Rose had held her so close — and when she departed, the glow Kathleen had been basking in was destroyed, leaving her feeling forsaken. She had pushed aside those ugly thoughts as she brushed her teeth, dressed and made her way to the factory.

Ignoring her responsibility to go immediately to work, she first stopped at Rose's machine.

Rose, her eyes full of mischief, asked, "How are you?"

"Much relieved now that I know that you got home all right." Kathleen shed her coat and draped it over her arm. She removed her hat and wiped a drop of rain from her face. It had been a damp walk this morning.

"I got home just fine," Rose said. She leaned toward Kathleen. "I whistled all the way."

Kathleen blushed. "Can we have lunch together?"

"Love to. Need to talk to you anyway."

"Get your ass to work!" Howe was moving in on them fast.

"See you later," Kathleen said.

Rose nodded and began sewing

Howe glared viciously at her. "What the hell you think you're doing, girlie, coming in and interrupting the girls who have sense enough to get in here early?"

"Just saying a pleasant hello to a friend," Kathleen answered. She flipped her coat from one arm to the other nearly hitting him in the face with it. "You ought to try being friendly sometime, Mr. Howe."

As though reprimanding a dog he said, "You watch your mouth, you damned old Irish washerwoman. You ain't all that important around here yet, and I don't expect you ever will be."

She had turned her back on him and was heading for the cloakroom when he slapped her bottom.

She would have struck him had a hand not stopped her midair. "Hey, nice hat you got, Kathleen. Let's see it." Bertha dragged her away from the howling floorwalker as he threatened to fire Kathleen on the spot. "Relax, Mr. Howe. Kathy here's just tired this morning. You know how women get during certain times of the month. That's all that's bothering her. She's a good worker and you know it."

Howe's eyes were large and fierce with anger. "I know she's a mouthy bitch, that's what I know."

"So am I," Bertha countered, "and you take it from me, so let her be just this once."

Bertha dragged her past the cloakroom as

Kathleen, fighting the strong arms, snarled, "I am *not* upset. I'm —"

Bertha brutally pinched her arm. "*Yes,* you are. Get to work. Now!" With firm control over the situation she virtually plunked Kathleen onto her stool.

Howe remained several rows away, but no longer yelling, and watched the two of them.

"Son of a bitch, that one," Bertha said. "I'd like to kill him. Don't you go starting anything around here, young lady." In hushed tones she cautioned Kathleen, "There's plans in the works. Don't you go making any problems. Join us or leave us, but no trouble from you."

"I've joined," Kathleen whispered. She had already begun to thread her machine. "Count on me."

"We'll see," Bertha said and moved off.

It took Kathleen most of the morning to cool off, but Bertha's warning had been firm. Something was going to happen very soon. Kathleen was afraid of a strike, afraid of losing her job and her apartment. She broke out in a sweat at the possibility, and her thoughts turned to Rose.

Throughout the day Kathleen glanced up from her work to look in Rose's direction. With all the machines blocking her view, she could not see her very well, but if she leaned to her right as if to reach for something, she could just make out Rose's profile.

At lunch they talked little, but Kathleen

137

recognized the importance of it. Things were very bad. Discussions between the employers and the workers were falling apart.

They sat quietly in front of Rose's machine, Kathleen recalling the previous night's scene over and over, her face growing warm, her lower belly taut. Rose grinned wider each time she looked up from her lunch.

"Keep your eyes sharp," Rose said at last, swallowing the final bite of her sandwich.

Kathleen was not sure she had heard her. "What?"

Rose brushed crumbs from her lap. "Talk to you later. Don't be late to work."

Kathleen felt as though she had been dismissed.

At one, the women were back at their machines. Kathleen noticed nothing out of the ordinary. At two, she checked her watch. Perhaps her edginess was because of Rose's quick dismissal after lunch, but Kathleen did not think so.

Suddenly, half the machines were turned off. The room was thick with tension as women, unspeaking, glanced at one another, their eyes critically observing others' reactions. As a body, nearly a hundred workers rose at once.

The strike! Kathleen had not been one of those told the exact time it would begin; she was only to join in when it did. The women walked quietly and in an orderly fashion to the cloakroom, gathered their hats, coats and pocketbooks and moved toward the door. By the dozens, the rest joined them.

Dumbstruck, Kathleen stared at over two hundred women funneling through the only exit available to them, knowing that she too was expected to stand with the rest, to leave her work pinned in the machine, to not do one more thing. She must strike.

On the floor above, Kathleen guessed, were another several hundred workers who were leaving.

Dobbs and the floor bosses were already yelling at the women. They stood screaming into their faces to get back to work. Spittle flew from their mouths as they hurled insults and threats at the workers.

No one slowed down; no one spoke. They had listened well to Richard Kent. He was a common laborer duly elected in the park as the man who would give directions to the workers when the strike occurred. He would state the dos and don'ts expected of them. Above all, he had said, no one was to retaliate in word or in deed.

Dobbs attempted to block their passage and was nearly flattened by the force of the women's bodies steadily moving as if a great machine had gone completely out of control. Trapped between the door casing and the rolling mass of humanity still coming at him, he screamed at them, cursed them and fired them all on the spot.

Silently, they continued moving past him and the floorwalkers, out the door and down the stairs. Disciplined and well mannered, they were careful not to provoke the men in any way.

Minna paused only long enough to say, "I'm sorry, Philip," as Jamison stared in disbelief at her, his eyes narrowed in pain and betrayal.

Kathleen shut off her machine, gathered her possessions and followed them. Somewhere was Rose.

Kathleen would find her and, working beside her, do whatever strikers did to make their conditions better. She wondered if she would ever have a job again.

Rose waited just beyond the entrance of the Asch Building and grabbed Kathleen as she exited. "There you are. Come on, it's time to start marching." They joined hundreds of women from the Triangle Shirtwaist Company, quietly singing hymns and already walking up and down the block.

Kathleen's excitement grew as she marched. Not five minutes passed before the police came, and there was her friend — indeed the friend of many of the women — Officer Patrick.

Several officers, Mr. Dobbs, Mr. Howe and Mr. Jamison took positions on the top step. At any moment, Kathleen expected Max Blanck and Isaac Harris, the Triangle's owners, to appear. The men stoically watched the marchers filing past.

Kathleen happened by when she heard Patrick say to Dobbs, "They're doing no harm, sir. They'll be back in the morning. Let them have their fling."

"Fling is it, Officer?" someone shouted. She pointed a bony finger at Dobbs. "You'll not see a one of us back there until management begins to listen to reason."

"Shut up, girl." Big and forceful Richard Kent, the union's organizer, marched with the strikers. He elbowed his way through the group toward the agitator. "It's your loud mouth, girl, that'll make them hate us and not take us seriously. Follow the marchers or leave the strike line."

The woman scowled fiercely at Kent as she moved on.

It was then that the strike fully hit Kathleen. "This is serious, isn't it?" she murmured to Rose.

"You didn't think this was a game, did you?" Rose replied.

"No, but I didn't think it would be like this."

"And how did you think it would be?" Placards on sticks were being passed through the crowd. Rose took two and handed one to Kathleen.

Kathleen swallowed hard. "I don't know. I guess I thought we'd all just go home and wait until the company came to its senses."

Rose laughed. "Not a chance. No, we've come to strike and to march. We've come to draw attention to ourselves, to make our needs known."

"What about tonight?" Kathleen asked quietly.

"Tonight we meet in the park and talk about what to do next. It'll be a long haul, I think."

"I mean about us." Kathleen looked at Rose's stern profile, unsmiling, almost scowling.

"I don't know. I'll be busy and so will you."

"So I should just wait?"

"Wait for what?"

Kathleen looked in disbelief at Rose. "Wait for us, for our romantic friendship."

Rose looked at the cobbles. "We are in a bad time, Kathleen. Our own timing ain't good. I want what you want, but I want to strike more, and that's going to take all me strength."

"You didn't really care about last night, did you?" Kathleen was whispering now. She was afraid of the strike and afraid of losing Rose without ever having had her. A single night? She wanted a string of nights.

"I'll be by your side each day and during night meetings, Kathleen. But you'll see that you'll have no energy for me."

"Impossible," Kathleen said. "Impossible."

"I'm sorry, darling." Rose whispered. "I'll be by your side, I say. Count on that."

That evening, there was a huge rally in the park up on east Fourteenth Street and University Place. Several hundred women and dozens of men, boys and girls were there. Countless candles lighted the evening. A man on a soapbox in the center of the group was speaking as Kathleen and Rose moved closer.

"We will back up the girls," he said, "and management will realize that it's not just girls that have concerns. The men do, too. We die younger, we work longer hours, we work harder."

Boos and angry shouts answered him.

"All right," he conceded to the overpowering women. "We work equally hard. But we're all poorly paid —"

"And I'm paid less because I'm a woman," a thin, small-boned woman shouted from the outside fringes of the circle. "That pisses me off plenty."

Loud shouts of agreement were scattered throughout the crowd.

"Get to the point," yelled a woman. "I didn't come here to discuss issues. We know what they are. How are we going to get them Goddamn bosses to listen to reason."

"Not by cursing them," someone answered.

"How, then?"

"We march," replied the soapbox spokesman. "We march until we drop, every day, all day, until they realize we mean business. We don't stop marching. If we're hungry, we march, if we're sick, we march, if we're cold, we march. We march until each and every one of us has what we want. Now who's with the union, and who's against it? Step away now. We're on the line at five tomorrow morning."

Nobody moved. Nobody disagreed. They were one body.

"Then five tomorrow morning," he said. "Go over to the swings. They got when everybody can sign up to march so's we can have a line from five A.M. to ten at night. We need caretakers for children and people to cook and take care of anybody who gets sick. Pitch in!"

On their way to sign for a duty, Kathleen asked Rose, "When will you march?"

Rose's face was set like a granite mask. "Morning till night until it's done. I'll cook and take care of kids. I'll do whatever is needed to do."

"Why do you work so hard?" Kathleen moved close enough so that their arms touched.

"I've worked for others all me life," she said through gritted teeth. "A boss is a boss. No matter who you work for, they make you feel like shit. I'm not going to feel like shit anymore. It's me way to get back at all the masters in the world. I hope to hell we strike for ninety-nine years."

Kathleen blinked, feeling the bitterness in Rose's words, remembering their conversation aboard ship: a new land, Rose had said, a new fight. She signed beneath whatever Rose had chosen to do.

The following morning, Kathleen met Rose in front of the Triangle Shirtwaist Company. Dozens had already arrived. Last evening she had asked

Rose to stay with her. Rose had refused, saying, "You'll need your strength, darling. Go home and go straight to bed."

She had, feeling utterly rejected.

Rose gave her a quick hug across her shoulders as they greeted each other. Her touch made Kathleen feel wanted again and less anxious that things might be slipping between them.

Those marching this morning picked up placards stating the union was on strike for better working conditions, better pay, shorter working hours, a cleaner factory. The line moved slowly, steadily, with no one rushing, no one pushing. People chatted and joked, feeling good about what they were doing. Not a single worker entered the Triangle.

At six the doors opened. Harris and Blanck were already there, their faces black as thunderclouds. Dobbs and the floorwalkers also appeared. The owners ignored the passing signs waving back and forth before them.

A woman directly in front of Kathleen stopped to address those on the steps. From somewhere Kent appeared.

"Keep moving," he warned. "You're out for a morning stroll. Nothing else."

Dobbs yelled at those nearest him, "Get to work. Nothing will happen to you if you go to work now."

As the line continued moving, Kent stepped forward. "That sounds like a threat, Mr. Dobbs."

"It ain't a threat, Kent." Dobbs whipped off his hat and struck it against his thigh. "I mean you won't be fired, and your pay won't be docked."

Kent moved wordlessly back into line.

Dobbs watched the line circling up and down Greene Street.

"To hell with you," he shouted. "I'll wait till noon. You better be back to work by then." He and the others went inside. Kathleen could see them watching from the tenth floor administrative offices.

The strikers marched until ten P.M., but nothing came from inside the factory. They marched for another three days without action from the owners. On the fourth day, three policemen, including Patrick, observed the line. The following day there were ten officers, the number increasing to thirteen within an hour.

The police moved cautiously amongst the crowd. Patrick sought out Kathleen and Rose. "Things could get rough, girls. I suggest you go back to work."

"Go to hell, Patrick," Rose answered. "This is America. I got a right to strike."

"Rose!" Kathleen said sharply. "Patrick has walked you home many a time. Don't speak so to him."

"Him walking me home at night don't make him me brother," Rose retorted.

Several yards ahead, Kathleen saw a woman fall to the street. A policeman quickly stepped out of the line. The victim was helped to her feet and continued walking. When Kathleen reached the spot, she saw blood on the pavement.

"Order," Kent was shouting as the marchers began to bunch up. "Order. Keep marching. Keep marching. This is an isolated incident."

The line thinned out and moved on.

"That's why I don't get friendly with the bobbies,"

Rose said, taking Kathleen's arm and pulling her away from Patrick and away from the blood. "He's on that side, we're on this. Right, Patrick?" she threw over her shoulder.

"It has to be this way," Patrick said. He looked sad and tired.

"And what are you doing for your mother?" Kathleen asked. He could not possibly be in favor of strong-arm tactics.

"They haven't walked out yet, but I expect they will. Goodbye, ladies. I must do me job."

"And we'll do ours," Kathleen said. She was surprised and deeply disappointed that he did not even look sorry that a woman had fallen. And she was very much aware that he never answered her question.

CHAPTER TWELVE

Monday, November 8, 1909

Rose and Kathleen had been on the strike line for five weeks. Kathleen now understood what Rose was trying to say in the beginning. Striking took all of her energy and then some.

Union dues were paying her rent now and that of many others. The dues were also feeding hundreds of families. Money was sent from sympathetic outside sources. Ladies of class and distinction had joined the strikers' cause. Some marched, some gave money, some gave services such as cooking, caring for the sick or for children — all so their parents could march.

Miss Mary Dreier of Brooklyn, President of the Women's Trade Union League, became deeply involved. Dreier had been arrested, then released only because she was wealthy. But she was scolded for not having told the authorities she was a friend of working girls. The incident caused a vast amount of publicity, drawing attention to the strike.

On the other side, prostitutes and thugs had moved in along with the policemen. Every day, Kathleen saw some striker arrested for supposedly having harassed an innocent bystanding woman or man who, in fact, had egged on the marcher until he blew.

Morning, noon and evening, there were meetings to encourage the strikers not to give in, not to give up. The company could not hold out forever. The strikers could!

"I repeat," a union leader was saying to the five A.M. group. "Keep calm. Don't antagonize. Don't sass anybody no matter how rough they get."

"What about my arm?" The man stood there tall and defiant, his arm in a sling.

"Don't sass anybody, John. I heard how that happened. I'm telling you, they're just looking for an excuse to thump you or to haul you off to jail."

"They got no cause to bust a man's arm," he snarled.

"That's right," the leader agreed. "And don't give them one, either. Let's go."

The group moved off. They no longer laughed the high-spirited laugh that was once so prevalent; talk had died to a minimum. They were tired and scared most of the time. Negotiations were at a standstill. People were looking for work elsewhere. There was some discussion about throwing in the towel.

Their early morning walks began in near darkness. It was becoming increasingly hard, Kathleen could tell, to motivate people to march. There was always the initial core group and then anyone else who would join in. Still, it was a large force, but not as large as when the strike had first begun.

This morning a man bumped into Kathleen, not apologizing. She moved aside to give him room. He was a tall fellow with a large belly. His hat was pushed back on his head, his coat open. Beneath it, he wore old pants and a faded shirt. Kathleen did not recognize him as a regular striker and was glad that new people were joining. She gave him a half-smile and continued on. When he bumped her again, she realized it was deliberate.

"Sir, back away please," she said.

"You smart-mouthing me?" In the weak morning light, his face looked cruel.

"No," she said, slightly exasperated. "You are deliberately hitting me. I'm asking you to stand away."

"Trouble, Kathleen?" Rose moved next to her. She had been talking with a couple of women a few feet back.

"What do you want, lady?" the man growled.

"He's pushing me on purpose," Kathleen said. "I've politely asked him to stand away." She stepped back.

Kent, who had not missed a single day's march

149

and was ever alert to strangers suddenly showing up, trotted up to them. "He's not a striker. He's a hired thug from the Triangle."

Belligerently, the man said, "You're breaking the law. You should be at your jobs."

Rose moved in close to him, but Kathleen slipped in front of her. "And I suppose pushing a lady around at five o'clock in the morning is a job."

The man bumped her with his great stomach, bouncing her into Rose.

"Damn you," Kathleen yelled at him. She flew at his face, scratching at him and delivering a cut to his unshaven cheek.

He slapped her hard once, and both Rose and Kent were on him. They pushed him to the ground. He received a blow or two before three policemen suddenly appeared and roughly pushed Kathleen, Rose and Kent toward a waiting wagon.

Unceremoniously, the police hurled them inside and drove them to the nearest jail. Dragged by their collars, they were hauled before a sleepy-eyed judge, the room already packed with others brought in late the previous day.

"Don't you people know enough to go to work?" the judge growled. "Sixty days!" His gavel came down hard enough to crack marble, and Kathleen and Rose found themselves being shoved along with dozens of other women toward cells in the rear of the building.

Inside, women cried or complained or screamed at their captors, and at the unjust treatment they were receiving. At ten A.M., they were released. Their bail had been posted, the union lawyer told them, by a very wealthy lady. Kathleen thought she caught the name Belmont, but was not sure. She had never heard of anyone named Belmont.

By 10:30, the women were back on the line.

For the length of Greene Street and the surrounding district, shops were picketed. If anyone wanted to buy anything on Greene, they had to first get through the line. Police and plainclothes detectives guarded the shops, their faces set, policemen with hands on their clubs, plainclothes men with their hands hanging loose and ready at their sides.

Rose threw up her arms, fists balled. "God, I hate this!"

Kathleen placed a calming hand on her. "The management says arresting us protects their rights. What about my rights?"

Rose's lips drew into a soft grin. "We've got time between five and eight tonight. Would you like to meet at your place?"

Kathleen felt a ringing impulse of hope. She had asked Rose a number of times to come home with her after their first romantic encounter. She had been refused so often, she stopped asking. Weeks had gone by.

"Yes," she said. They sealed their agreement with smiles.

At noon, volunteers passed out pretzels, apples and hot tins of coffee for lunch. More arrests were made; more women disappeared only to reappear some hours later. The women were afraid of the police and the thugs who had increased in numbers as the day wore on, but they kept calm and did their job.

By five, Kathleen's head was splitting. She

walked with tired steps to the waiting union leaders who would boost their morale at the end of the long day's efforts. Rose, a few feet ahead of her, chatted with Bertha.

At the brief meeting Kathleen listened with deaf ears, wanting only to lie down beside Rose.

"You going home with Rose?"

Standing beside Kathleen was Abigale Yakowec, first-generation American with hardly a trace of a Polish accent. Abigale had worked on the floor above Kathleen. She was petite and bouncy with flashing brown eyes. Her hair was bobbed, her hat flamboyant. She wore plain clothing in sharp contrast to her bonnet and enthusiastic personality. She was known as the driving spirit of the strike. Her boundless energy persevered even above and beyond that of the union leaders. Abigale was there to calm and soothe the walkers, encouraging them not to curse or vent anger, not to lose hope. She had not missed a day's walk since the strike began.

Kathleen liked Abigale, her endless vitality and good wishes. "Actually Rose is coming home with me."

"I heard her ask you." Abigale leaned toward Kathleen. "Did you know that she's inclined toward romantic relationships?" A sense of unease settled over Kathleen. "She's known as having had several," Abigale said.

She looked genuinely dismayed, but that only angered Kathleen. "And how would you know?"

"It's general knowledge. I've talked to her about it."

Kathleen's words were sudden and sharp. "And just what business is it of yours, Abigale?"

152

"None, except my concern for your soul as a fellow Catholic. Rose told me she doesn't care about hers."

"I don't know what you're talking about. Actually, I don't care what you think."

She turned her back on Abigale who said, "I'm sorry I've angered you, Kathleen. You're a nice girl. I'd hate to see your soul damaged."

Kathleen whirled on Abigale. "How? How will my soul be damaged?"

"By having a romantic relationship."

Rose joined them. "Preaching again, Abigale?"

"You won't listen," Abigale said.

"Neither will I," Kathleen said. "I've committed no sin. Neither has Rose."

"Corinthians, Chapter Six, Verse Nine. 'Wrong-doers will never possess the kingdom of God, no sexual pervert.' "

Rose pushed back her bonnet, the better to glare at Abigale. "Me mum taught me Scripture, too." She stepped closer to her adversary. "Exodus Twenty, Chapter Thirteen, Sixth Commandment. Rose, thou shall not kill do gooders."

Kathleen smirked as Abigale's eyes raked her. Abigale looked at Rose. "Yes, that sounds like someone on the outside of God. But I tell you again, Rose, romantic relationships are a sin against nature." She made the sign of the cross.

"How the hell would you know? Bet you read, don't you? You'd have to to get such insane notions." Her face was only inches from Abigale's. "The real sin is that these poor bastards —" Her eyes never left Abigale's as she gestured to the strikers. "— have to slave and starve for factory owners who become so rich off them that they'll never know a day's hunger. They don't pay their workers enough to eat on or to buy decent clothing for their families. And how many have died because of factory conditions? You're a factory worker, you little twit. You should know this."

"I don't disagree with that, and you know it," Abigale said. "It's what you are that's wrong."

Rose gave her a rough push. "That's enough, lady."

Kathleen stepped between them. "Cut it out, Rose. Abigale, take your prattling tongue and be off with you." She swung Rose around and pulled her away from Abigale.

Rose's face was set like stone. "Bitch!" she snarled.

Kathleen yanked hard at Rose's sleeve. "Come on."

Rose angrily straightened her hat and yanked at her coat. "God, I hate self-righteous people."

Kathleen kept her hand on Rose's sleeve all the way to her apartment. Inside, she took their coats and tossed them over a chair. In minutes, she had made tea and slapped a cup in Rose's hand. The lantern burned bright on the table. Rose, silent and brooding, slurped her tea, muttering obscenities.

Kathleen sat across from Rose, watching the highlights dance in her smoldering eyes. "You're very beautiful," she said. "Even when you're angry."

Rose gave her a disgusted look.

"You are. I don't know why you let Abigale make you mad. She doesn't know what she's talking about."

A sin against nature, Abigale had said. Kathleen

would ask Father Michael the next time she went to confession and just clear the whole thing up. Likely, he would tell her she had committed no sin. She was sure he would say that. She had told herself that many times lately. Many, many times.

"Come," she said. She was without guilt, wanting only for Rose to hold her, love her. This was love, not just a romantic relationship. "Romantic relationship" sounded transitory, without substance, especially if Kathleen was the only woman in Rose's life. "Come and lie down with me." A pleasurable shock streaked through her thighs and up through her belly and chest.

Rose set down her cup and let Kathleen lead her to the bed. "I don't know why I let Abigale trouble me," she said. They sat beside each other.

"She has nothing better to do," Kathleen said, pushing Rose back and climbing in next to her.

"We have to be up and gone by eight," Rose said.

Kathleen put her lips against Rose's ear. "I don't care about that right now. I don't care about Abigale or the strike. I don't even care if I end up starving. All I want right now is you — without worry, without sadness, in fact, without clothing on, like we did the last time."

Rose laughed. Seductively, she began to pull the pins from Kathleen's hair. It tumbled in heavy handfuls into Rose's face, making her laugh louder.

Kathleen shook her head, freeing the rest of her hair. "There, see? Isn't this much better than anything outside these doors?"

"Yes," Rose whispered.

With maddening slowness, they undressed each other. They sat cross-legged on the bed, face to face.

155

"You're so beautiful, Kathleen."

Kathleen dropped her eyes to Rose's pale blond tangle, reaching in a line up to her navel. Gray grew there too. Kathleen had not noticed before. Hereafter, she would look at Rose's hair and remember this lovely view.

A musky, delicious odor hit her. She felt a surge of wetness as she shifted her position.

Simultaneously, they touched each other. "Good Lord," Kathleen managed to whisper. She heard Rose murmuring as through a fog, felt fingertips touch her nipple. Fire ripped her in two.

Her hand shook as she touched Rose's breast. Rose bent to kiss her arm and to rest her head against it. "I don't ever think I've felt like this before."

Doubt crept into their intimacy. "Shhh, don't talk." Kathleen did not need to be reminded that there had been others before her.

They stroked each other's breasts while sliding a finger in that warm, wet place that Kathleen was sure was Earth's heaven. She followed Rose, moving her finger to the left and to the right, and up and down just as Rose did. She heard Rose suck in a deep breath. Beneath her fingers, Kathleen felt Rose's nipple harden, watched it point straight at her. She became dizzy, heard another sharp intake of breath and discovered it was her own.

They were close now, Rose the leader, Kathleen the follower. "I don't know how long I can wait — or sit here," Rose struggled to say.

A burning sensation built within Kathleen. "I'm there, darling Rose, I'm there." She was not there, but she thought she was, and then Rose threw back her head. Her hand moved rapidly against Kathleen. Inside her body, Kathleen tightened her muscles thinking a hot iron was pressing against her.

Rose was gasping, Kathleen was gasping. Their hands continued moving until Kathleen straightened her legs. She fell backward, Rose following her, their hands still locked on each other. They let go, and with vise-like grips clung to each other.

Rose fell across Kathleen's thigh, pushing a leg against her crotch. She rocked against Kathleen as Kathleen answered in rhythm. They clutched each other until the bones of Kathleen's thin body became painful.

Tears welled up in Kathleen's eyes. She buried her face in the deep hollow of Rose's shoulder and wept.

"Oh, honey, it's all right. It's all right." Rose rocked her back and forth, whispering soothing words in her ear.

Kathleen could not remember ever feeling such deep grief. And why grief? The thought brought fresh tears. She held Rose, intending never to let her go.

They slept in each other's arms until it was time to rise. By then Kathleen's tears had stopped. Never once did Rose say, "I love you," and how hard Kathleen had prayed that she would.

CHAPTER THIRTEEN

Monday, November 22, 1909

Kathleen and Rose reached the strikers' meeting late having taken a quick nap before leaving. It left Kathleen tired and unwilling to leave the bed. What finally got them moving was when she looked around the dark, depressing room and saw nothing of beauty that she owned. Not a dress, not a coat, not a picture, not even a dried flower in a discarded jar.

"We're sweatshop workers, Rose. Will we always be sweatshop workers? Will I never own a pretty thing again?"

Rose rolled out of bed immediately, tears in her eyes. "Yes, damn it, you will if I have anything to say about it."

Kathleen plumped the pillow under her head and said, "I saw you give away your pretty hat the other day. It must have cost you fifty cents. Why did you do that?"

Rose sighed and sat back down beside her. She leaned over and kissed her nose. "I believe," she said quietly, "that if you have something that means a lot to you and somebody else likes it very much, you should give it away."

Kathleen sat up in protest. "Why, that's stark crazy, Rose. You don't have enough pretty things and certainly nothing to give away."

Rose pulled on a stocking. "It ain't that I don't want the thing for myself. It's that they want it just as much."

"Then let them buy it for themselves."

Rose straightened her slip and reached for her dress. "It's in the giving, Kathleen, darling."

"A waste of money from a poor woman, if you ask me." Kathleen spoke sharply.

"I didn't ask you, love, and I won't."

"You're peculiar."

"That may be true. But peculiar or not, we've got to rise. You and I are sweatshop girls. I'm sick of being poor." She buttoned another button and signaled Kathleen to get out of bed.

"If you were rich, you'd still have nothing," Kathleen said, boldly slapping Rose's bottom.

They laughed as they finished dressing.

Packed into the Great Hall at Cooper Union where half a century earlier, Abraham Lincoln had criticized the spread of slavery, people sat or stood along the huge room's sides, filling every available space. The strike was spreading to other factories, and there was talk it might spread to other cities.

Overflow meetings were simultaneously being held at Beethoven Hall, Manhattan Lyceum and Astoria Hall. In the Great Hall, people listened quietly and intently as speaker after speaker listed grievances. A woman described her being jailed because she had been talking in the picket line, and likely she would be jailed again because she wasn't about to stop talking. A man Kathleen recognized from weeks ago told how a thug had broken his arm. A second man gave a similar story. Several more speakers listed their complaints before the union's officers were presented.

Mary Dreier spoke of abhorrent conditions in the shops. And then Samuel Gompers, President of the American Federation of Labor, was introduced. People leaped to their feet, the vast crowd wildly cheering him. Several minutes passed before they allowed him to speak.

"I want you men and women not to give all your enthusiasm for a man, no matter who he is. I prefer you put your enthusiasm into the cause of your union." His deep voice carried easily throughout the cavernous room. There was sadness in his tone when he announced that he had never before declared a strike. He had done his share to prevent strikes, he said. "But there comes a time when not to strike is nothing more than riveting chains of slavery upon our wrists." He spoke bitterly when he talked about the inconvenience to shirtwaist manufacturers. "There are things more important than your profit. There are the lives of the boys and girls, the men and the women."

A voice cried out from the audience. "I wish to say a few words." Clara Lemlich, a small, frail woman who was badly beaten by ruffians during a strike in Louis Leiserson's shop, was lifted to the stage. Her flashing black eyes took in the audience. Kathleen was mesmerized.

Straining to hear, she leaned forward as Lemlich said, "I have no more patience for talk. I feel and suffer from the things we grieve about. I am ready to strike now."

En masse the audience rose. The cheering was ear splitting. The strike was on; grim faces filled with determination declared war.

"Our new fight," Rose said, as the din settled and other speakers continued. "The big one."

The following day, people wanting to join the union went to Clinton Hall where they stood in lines thirty and forty feet deep to sign on. Speakers in Yiddish, Italian and English staffed the tables. Women without work — confused, frightened, excited — put hand to pen and paid a quarter in dues. Fraught with strike fever as grievances were aired and informative handbills were passed out, the union swelled.

Kathleen and Rose were about to leave when a squat man, his deep-set eyes full of fire, grabbed Kathleen by the arm. "You speak English?" he demanded. "You a union member? Can you read?"

Before she could think to protest his roughness she had answered yes.

"Go sit down over there and sign up those women." He shoved a stack of forms at her and spun her toward an empty table where dozens waited to become union members. When she glanced back again to tell him there was no way she could do this job, he was gone.

"Go to it, darling," Rose said. "You're in union work now."

"What are you going to do?" Kathleen asked.

"Why, help you, of course."

"Thanks," Kathleen said, grateful for this wonderful person beside her. It was so like Rose to help her. She always had, whenever Kathleen had let her.

The paperwork was easy enough to handle. She assisted those who could not read, filling in their names, addresses and birth dates if they knew it. Others completed their own. Every few minutes a woman with a Women's Trade Union League silk banner worn across her chest came around and collected the dues money.

Kathleen worked an hour or so before things slowed down. Tomorrow, she thought, tomorrow there'll be no fooling around. Even with having landed in jail once, she expected things were going to get far worse before they ever got better.

* * * * *

The strike was on in earnest. Day by day, week by week, it sapped Kathleen's energy. She worried incessantly about money, food, the coming winter. There was no work except for scabs. They were better protected than the strikers who did nothing more than walk up and down Greene Street.

Activities, both bad and good, were increasing for the strikers. In the Essex Market court house, Magistrate Krotel fined five shirtwaist makers who had been part of a riot ten dollars each. He threatened them with the workhouse if they showed up before him again. Magistrate Breen at Jefferson Market fined several more women for annoying nonunion girls going to work. Policemen and plainclothed men guarding strike breakers listened to curses and threats as they ushered the scabs to and from the factories. Shops lining Greene Street and surrounding blocks continued to be picketed.

A group of women, Kathleen and Rose included, agreed to picket the J. Brown shop on Wooster Street just below Broome Street.

For the first ten minutes, no one bothered them. No one came close to them. Then, as if out of nowhere, a gang of tough-looking young men ran out of the store and into the fifteen women, pushing and pulling at them.

"You ain't got no right to be bothering this man's shop," a bearded youth shouted in Kathleen's face. He pushed her hard enough to make her stumble into the woman behind her.

The shop owner shouted at them from his door, "Move faster, you gilded women, and walk on down the sidewalk. You got no right to be blocking this doorway. I'll have you thrown in the gutter. Girls,

163

bah!" He continued badgering them as the thugs screamed insults into the women's ears.

Three police officers, their hands on their clubs, watched from one side, waiting for one of the women to break the law. Rose did. She swung at a tough.

He pushed her hard and tripped, landing on her as she went down. He was a big man, much bigger than Rose, who tried to force him off her. Even he seemed surprised at their encounter, attempting to disentangle himself from her flailing arms and long skirt that had somehow wrapped itself around his legs.

"Damn you, lady!" he screeched. "Lemme be, you she-devil." She slapped his face as he rose.

"That's it, you bunch of fools," an officer shouted. "Get in the wagon."

In minutes, Kathleen, Rose and the rest were on the way to jail.

"I didn't attack him. He attacked *me!*" Rose yelled at the police. It took a man on either side of her to get her into the wagon, and a sharp blow to the side of her head with a club to keep her there.

"You people go back to work, you won't be getting hurt." The officer slammed the door on the screaming, protesting women. He struck the caged window once where hands gripped it, nearly smashing several fingers pulled out of the way just before the stick landed.

In jail, they slept huddled together on four cots in a single cell. They were fed scant meals of thin slices of meat, once or twice a potato and stale coffee. They cried and complained and soothed one another, indignation and bitterness oozing from their pores. They shared a potty bucket and learned the first day that modesty was not the most important thing in the world for women. Unity was.

Three days later and many meals short, they were released with severe warnings not to be seen near Wooster Street again. It did not stop them. The following day, they were back and so were several more. Surprisingly, women of class were showing up in the picket lines. Kathleen eyed their fine garments of shimmering greens and blues, their beautiful hats decorated with colorful feathers. Eventually, she met Elsie Coke, Elizabeth Dutcher and Violet Pike. They went to Vassar, they told her. She did not know what Vassar was, but apparently it was an important place, for the young women were definitely well-to-do.

Sometimes six hundred strikers at a time were arrested while scores were sent to the workhouse, and still the strike went on. Money poured in from supporting shop owners, rich bystanders and individuals who had suffered and were now better off. Food was donated and distributed. Rents continued to be paid through union dues. Somehow the cause was kept alive and basic needs seen to.

Kathleen heard of an unusual support group that had formed. A mansion was deeded by a mother to her daughter so that the young lady could sit in court day after day and with a mortgage, bail out arrested girls as soon as bail had been set. J.P. Morgan's daughter, Anne, attended a demonstration given in honor of a destitute girl who had returned from the workhouse. Mrs. O.H.P. Belmont, mother of the Duchess of Marlborough, spent a night in court and at three A.M. gave her Madison Avenue mansion as security for the appearance of the arrested strikers in court the following day.

With wealthy women beginning to join the union's cause and to march in its ranks, the thugs and policemen backed off. To arrest one of these women or the daughters of these women was a grave error, and no one wanted to lose their jobs, especially not the policemen who enjoyed the power of their position.

Kathleen managed to sleep beside Rose most evenings at the Wooster Street apartment, but they did not make love anymore. Almost as soon as their heads hit the pillow, they were asleep. Kathleen rarely completed her prayers, but she always got through the one she thought most important, that of the Lord's Prayer, ending with a plea for the good Lord to bless her love for Rose. Pangs of concern and guilt were beginning to nag at her. She was actually glad that she and Rose were not making love. She did not then have to deal with the right and wrong of it.

Before confession one Saturday evening, in the dim light of a candle, she sat in a rear pew and pored over a Bible the young parish priest had loaned her. She saw several places where she could prove Abigale's words to be true. St. Paul was the worst of them all. He did not go on at great length, but the message was clear. As she reread the passage several times, she wished Paul were not so cogent. She went to confession, but froze at the last minute without asking her question: was it all right to love Rose or was it, indeed, wrong.

Tonight, lying in Rose's arms, her concerns were

especially strong in her mind. She wanted to get the thing settled. If she was wrong, she and Rose could live together as sisters. If she was not wrong, then she could completely open her heart and give more of herself. She had always held some part of herself in reserve.

She woke grumpy and snapped at Rose for not getting up right away. She brushed her hair angrily and cursed as her fingernails snagged her stockings.

"What's the matter with you?" Rose asked. She always awoke with a smile. She smiled now, amused at Kathleen's struggle with her slip.

"Oh, don't look so silly, Rose. It doesn't become you." Her brogue was thick, a sure sign of her displeasure.

Rose pulled Kathleen to her breast. "We haven't been together in weeks. You need it. I need it."

Kathleen's eyes flared. "I'm not some animal who needs it." She pushed Rose aside and reached for her shoes.

Rose chuckled at Kathleen's discomfort. "Well, ain't we in a mood? It sounds to me like you need it. Animal or not, I know when I need a good loving, and I need a good loving, and you're just the woman who can do it."

Kathleen grabbed the teapot. "Am I? Am I the woman who can love you? By what right can I love you? Who said? Where does it say it's all right to love you? And how can I love you? Can I kiss you? Can I truly take you in my arms and hold you like a man would hold you? Touch you like a man would? I can't even lie on top of you and do to you what a man would do. Is that love, or is it just lying on top of you? You pant and thrash around, but aren't I supposed to be *in* you to make it count? Isn't that what the Bible is talking about?"

Rose sat up, stung. "What are you talking about, girl? Where'd all this nonsense come from? That ragpicker Abigale's filled your head full of trash. *Trash,* do you hear me?" She walked over and ripped the pot from Kathleen's hand. "And what the hell is this about lying on top of me like a man? You don't even feel like a man, ain't built like a man, ain't heavy enough or hairy enough or hard enough. That's exactly why I want a woman. I don't want a hard rod up me hole. I want a soft woman's hand. Her finger, lass." She bent close to Kathleen's face. "Two if you will, maybe even three on a real hot night. You can do that better than any man's rod up me legs. And what's more —" She threw the pot across the room. It landed with a clatter against the opposite wall. "— it feels better. Hell, I've slept with me share of men. Some by force, some because I let them. They can't hold a penny candle to you, love, not even a million-dollar candle." Her voice softened. "I never told you before, Kathleen that I love you. I'm in love with you like if I was a man. I wasn't ready to say that before. I was afraid. You know that there were other women I saw while I saw you. That is, until I started coming here every night . . ."

Kathleen heard the words she had longed to hear from Rose. She wanted to say to her, *Oh, darling, and I love you, too.* But her anger froze her tongue, and she said instead, "Sure, and Abigale made it plain you slept with others. She *knew* it."

Rose pulled Kathleen closer. "Damn her soul, too. A little Miss Busybody, that one. Probably pissed because she ain't getting any."

"She's a religious lady."

"She's a self-righteous, cold-hearted woman, Kathleen, and we both know it. She goes around trying to make everybody feel better about the strike, and how it's really a holy cause, and we ought to not lose courage. All that's good, but we could still march on without her interfering in our lives. I can see she's set your mind awhirl."

Kathleen tucked her head beneath Rose's chin. "I read in the Bible about St. Paul."

"What's he know? He never even got married, to me knowledge. What can he know about love, about body love? Most people like body love. If he never got any body love, how could he ever tell if it was good or bad? What nonsense!"

"Is it nonsense?"

"Aye, it is. Pure nonsense."

"Is kissing you bad?"

"Good heavens, darling, none of it's bad. Put that thought out of your head right now."

Rose's anger made Kathleen's stomach knot up into a tight little ball. She did not want Rose to be angry. Kathleen might lose her. She did not want to lose her. She would go to confession Saturday evening and talk to Father Michael. He would clear everything up in a whit.

CHAPTER FOURTEEN

Wednesday, December 1, 1909

The strike was still on. In bitterly cold weather, people walked bundled up, unrecognizable in thick scarves, heavy coats and shoes. They marched patiently and doggedly from morning to night, seven days a week. Food was scarce, money more scarce, but morale was still holding its own. There were those who continued working tirelessly, encouraging people not to return to work until their demands were met. Scabs had filled hundreds of jobs, but not enough to satisfy consumer demand. Thousands of workers were needed to do that. In addition, it was becoming tougher for scabs to cross picket lines. Shirtwaist work was being sent to other cities to be completed. Strikers were becoming ugly, tired of delays, tired of the length of the strike and tired of lack of cooperation on the part of management.

In the sumptuous gymnasium of the Colony Club — New York's most exclusive club, Kathleen had heard — four hundred wealthy women sat in gilt chairs and listened to stories from strikers who had been invited for a tea and to relate their experiences. Ten girl strikers, some mere children, were specifically brought to the club by Mary Dreier, still the Women's Trade Union League's president. No girl's name was given for fear of retaliation.

On December third, a parade of ten thousand striking waistmakers marched four abreast down Broadway to City Hall and called upon Mayor McClellan. They wished to present him with a petition in the name of thirty thousand women regarding protests against abuse and mistreatment at the hands of his police force. They reached City Hall Park at 2:30 P.M. They were barred by mounted police and had to wait on Park Row while Mayor McClellan accepted the petition from a lone woman, Miss Marot, the group's representative.

"Son of a bitch is afraid we'll attack him," Rose said.

"There's no man afraid of just one woman," Kathleen answered. "Ten thousand's a different story."

Two days later, the Political Equality Association, with Mrs. O.H.P. Belmont's help, rented the

Hippodrome. Kathleen and Rose got there early enough before angry, frustrated police began turning others away. Inside, baskets were passed and a healthy collection of money was raised to aid the needy. On December ninth, Kathleen and Rose attended another mass meeting held in the Thalia Theatre by the Socialists of New York.

The Grand Central Palace was filled to overflowing on the thirteenth to hear a report by John Mitchell and Morris Hillquit on the arbitration conference. President Taft himself, they told the crowd, had said that all right-minded men recognized the union as necessary in modern industrialism. Hillquit told of a fake union leader who, for three thousand dollars, would show management how to break up and sell out the entire Shirtwaist Makers' Union.

More mass meetings were held with Kathleen and Rose attending as many as possible. More money poured in. Ministers of God began preaching about the strike from the pulpit, saying, "Don't give in. Don't give up." On December eleventh, riots had begun on Clinton Street. At Arlington Hall, medals were presented by a committee of Socialist women, to girls who had been sent to the workhouse. In a single day, forty-five thousand issues of the *Call*, New York's daily left-wing paper, representative of the interests of labor, were sold at eight cents apiece by girls and women wearing banners declaring themselves union members.

"Give me one of those banners," Kathleen said to the leader. "I'll sell your papers for you." Both she and Rose did, their teeth chattering all day. The weather was freezing, but it did not stop them.

"The weather won't stop us, either," one of several coatless girls told Kathleen. "I can't even afford a coat." For the rest of the day, Kathleen, Rose and the others shared their coats.

Christmas day was a happy one for Kathleen and Rose. They did not strike. Instead, Kathleen went to mass and Rose stayed in bed. The previous day they had pooled seventy-five precious cents and splurged on a half chicken and two potatoes each. Christmas afternoon they relished their simple meal and laughed uproariously as they licked their plates clean.

For gifts they had agreed to spend no more than a nickel on each other. Kathleen gave Rose a gilded golden chain. Rose gave Kathleen a heart-shaped locket. They combined the two gifts and took turns wearing them, greatly admiring how the chain and locket looked on each other.

They were on the line again the following day, but on January first, 1910, everyone rested, those striking and those fighting the strikers. Kathleen lay snuggled deeply in blankets and in Rose's arms. "At least they have brains enough to relax one day."

"Bless them," Rose said. "I have unfinished business." She rolled over on top of Kathleen who pulled Rose's lips to her own.

They hauled themselves out of their warm bed on January second to make their way to Carnegie Hall. Three hundred and seventy women previously arrested and fined or sent to the workhouse sat on the stage wearing banners across their chests that read *Arrested* or *Workhouse Prisoner*. They told their stories. Packed somewhere in the middle of the overflowing audience Kathleen and Rose listened in captivated attention.

On January seventeenth at the breakfast table, Kathleen read several positive columns from the *Call*, to Rose.

"Sounds like the newspapers are becoming pretty sympathetic," Rose commented.

"It gets better," Kathleen said. "Some of the bosses housed their scabs overnight in the Bijou Waist Company up on Broadway. They put a large police guard out front to prevent voluntary desertion that the scabs have begun."

Within a week there was, at last, a settlement. It took several days for all the shirtwaist makers' companies to settle, but settle they did. On January twenty-third, in the Grand Central Palace, two thousand unionists celebrated throughout the night.

They left the Palace to march four, five and six abreast all the way up to Broadway and back again, Kathleen and Rose right in the thick of it. They sang victory songs and shouted fighting slogans. People in upper-story apartments threw open their windows and cheered them on.

Returning jubilantly to the Palace, handbills were passed out listing their successes. Kathleen read that they had won a fifty-two-hour week, a raise in wages from twelve to fifteen percent, the elimination of subcontracting in factories and homes. Night work was limited to two hours per day and not more than twice a week. Legal holidays would now be paid for, and in the slack season, work would be divided among all the workers instead of a few.

Kathleen was thrilled as she read the list, but still she was concerned. She fought her way through the crowd searching out Richard Kent who was being praised as one of the great strike men on the line. Holding the handbill out to him, she asked, "What about cleanliness, toilet rooms, a larger working space for each factory worker?"

"There's more work to be done, Kathleen," he said.

CHAPTER FIFTEEN
Thursday, January 23, 1910

———

Kathleen left the Palace early. She should have stayed with Rose, doing what Rose was doing: singing, dancing and hugging everyone in sight. They celebrated the successful conclusion of their months of work, their part in the largest women's strike force in all of America, their efforts at helping win the strike. They had better conditions, more money — and greatest of all, their love for each other.

She should have been out of her mind with happiness, but she had not yet talked to Father Michael, putting off her religious concerns regarding romantic relationships until the strike had ended. She thought it impossible to deal with both problems at once. Now it was time.

Yes, she should have continued celebrating. But she was a good girl of Ireland; she believed in all that was correct and proper. She was seized by a tremendous sense of duty to her soul to straighten things up right away. The weight of her problem seemed so great that she thought it better to feign exhaustion and just go on home, rather than to allow her depression to dampen the evening. Somehow Rose had believed her, kissed her quickly on the cheek and was swallowed by the crowd before Kathleen had gone five feet.

The following Saturday evening, Rose walked her to confession. "Why do Catholics confess their sins to a man?" she asked.

Kathleen stayed close to Rose's side. "We don't confess to a man."

"A priest, then."

"Not a priest either. The priest is a representative of Christ. We confess to Christ through the priest."

"Can't you just talk directly to Christ without a middleman?"

Kathleen laughed. "Not in the Catholic Church you can't. There are times when I'd like to, though." She thought of the question she would ask this evening, the answer she hoped to receive.

They stopped before the large, opulent church. "Goodness, this is something," Rose said, looking up at the stately columns. "I was in here briefly not long ago to get out of the cold. This is a rich church."

"It is," Kathleen said. She started up the stone steps.

"Bleeding the poor dry to run it, ain't they?"

Kathleen's temper flared. "Don't you be running my church into the ground, Rose Stewart. You don't even go to church."

"I don't need to, lass. I talk to the Lord straight on."

Vexed, Kathleen replied, "And I'm sure He hears you faster than me, and better. And probably louder."

"No, He hears me just like He hears you. I just don't do all you do and pay money to do it."

"My money helps to run this church and feed the poor."

"They feed you lately?" Rose stood on the sidewalk, head cocked.

Kathleen wanted to argue with her, to tell Rose she was out of order. It was her duty, and her honor, to contribute every week to the collection. It was a rich church attended by a lot of poor and rich who gave what they could. "Oh, never mind," she snapped. "I've a confession to give."

"All right, I apologize," Rose said.

She left Rose waiting and entered the pillared church. It was dark and cold inside. Pews stretched in long rows from front to back. She blessed herself with holy water from a marble font just inside the door. Halfway down the aisle, she genuflected and slid into a pew. She knelt and prayed. There were several people in line waiting to give their confessions. She would organize her thoughts before joining them.

A half an hour later she pushed aside the curtain to the confessional and knelt.

The confessional was divided into three sections, each approximately nine square feet with each entrance concealed by a heavy purple drape extending from top to bottom. The priest occupied the middle section; sinners knelt singularly in the side sections on a hard wooden step. Into each wall adjacent to the priest was a small wooden window at eye level. It was drilled full of holes and covered with a sliding partition drawn back when the priest was ready to listen.

Kathleen waited, hearing the whisperings of Father Michael speaking to whomever was confessing. Beads of sweat popped out on her forehead as her hands began to tremble. She chided herself for her fear. She was here only to go to confession, something she did every week. She was also here to ask a question, *that* question. She rephrased it several different ways as she had been doing for weeks. She was not comfortable with any of her choices. She would just have to rely on the good Lord to put the proper words in her mouth when the time —

The window slid back, revealing Father Michael's shadowy figure. He leaned toward her, sighing deeply. She could picture him saying mass on the altar, his ruddy, puffy cheeks, the long hairs growing from his nostrils, his fat bald head, the richly embroidered vestments heavily laden with thick gold and silver piping, swaying on his large girth as he moved from one side of the altar to the other.

She made the sign of the cross while saying, "Bless me, Father, for I have sinned. It has been one week since my last confession." The priest sighed again, sounding a bit bored, she thought.

She listed her usual: she had fallen asleep every night while saying her evening prayers, she had said "damn" four times and "hell" six. She had become angry at least fifteen times. Daily, she had wished ill will toward her floorwalkers and toward Mr. Dobbs.

She continued for a few seconds more, then the priest said, "For your penance, say three Hail Marys and three Our Fathers."

She saw him make the sign of the cross, indicating her absolution. He began to draw the small partition.

"Wait, Father," she said in a loud whisper. The door paused.

"Is there something else, my daughter?"

Again she detected a note of boredom — perhaps tiredness — in his voice. His hurry to cut her off strengthened her resolve to ask about romantic love, about how much was allowed to occur between two women. She drew herself straighter, stiffer.

"It's a question I have, Father. I need some advice."

"Can you come to the Rectory?"

"I can't. I have no time."

He sighed again, but she pushed onward. "I like to kiss this woman I know."

"That is no sin, my child. Go in peace." Again the door began to close.

"Father, I like to kiss her on the lips."

The door continued to slide.

"I like to touch her private places."

The door stopped, then slowly reopened.

"Private places?"

"Yes, Father. I wondered ... if there was a problem with that. We do no harm. We only touch each other."

"How?"

"How?" She hadn't expected he would want to know how, only that they did.

"How?" he asked again.

"I don't know if that's important, Father, only if there is a concern on your part."

"My daughter," he said in a patient voice. "I cannot help you if I don't fully understand how it is that you touch each other."

"With our hands mostly," she responded. The sweat that had first covered her forehead now ran down the sides of her face. More was snaking its way down her ribcage.

"And just how with your hands?"

She shrugged. "I don't know, Father. We just touch each other. I put my hand on her, she puts hers on me."

"Do you use fingers to ..." His voice trailed off.

She closed her eyes. "Yes," she answered bluntly.

"And do you move your fingers around on each other?"

"Yes."

"Do you reach ..." He hesitated. "... a climax?"

She had wondered what it was called. "Yes."

"And do you touch her . . . breasts too?"

"I do, Father." She was uncomfortable with his inquisitiveness. She was a modest woman. She had not thought he would ask about such intimacy regarding her private life. God already knew. She was here only for a simple question: was it right to touch Rose? Was it wrong?

"You sound very involved with this . . . woman." He sounded gruff.

"I am, Father, and I wondered what the Lord would think. I think I know, but I'm not sure."

"And what do you think He believes, my child?"

"He may care if I'm hurting my friend. He doesn't care if I'm not."

"But you are hurting her, daughter."

Kathleen felt a rush of fear. Hurting Rose? How?

He said, "You are not allowing her to become a wife. You are not allowing her to bear children, which is every woman's primary function in life."

"To bear children? That's my primary function in life, to bear children?"

"Of course," he said kindly. "That's what you are for. That's what you do. It's a beautiful thing," he told her. "Women are the only ones who can bear little ones, soldiers of Christ. The more, the better. If you can have several children, if your friend has several, think of all the souls there are for heaven when they die."

"I wouldn't have children with the thought in mind of them dying, Father," she said. "My friend is not interested in having children nor in having a husband. She wants me and has no trouble with the idea of me being her wife — or husband — or however she would think of me, and I feel the same way except for this question. I wanted to know how you thought the Lord felt."

"That is how He feels, my dear. He wants you to get married to some fine young man and have as many children as you can have during your childbearing years. It's a wonderful thing you're able to do."

"I'm not ready for marriage, Father." She felt herself sinking into a severe depression and rested her head against the screen.

"Some women never are, but still they marry and have large and wonderful families."

"But, Father, are they happy?"

"It is not for a woman to be happy or unhappy, my daughter. It is her purpose to bear souls for God and for the Church. Your involvement with this other woman prevents either of you from fulfilling your true purpose in life. Your other choice is to become a nun."

A nun! Not likely. She had known since she was young that it was not her calling.

Her knees were beginning to hurt; her chest ached with an inexplicable pain centered in her breastbone. She had a terrible headache. And Rose waited outside.

"Thank you, Father. You've been a big help." His counsel had destroyed her life. She could no longer hold Rose, kiss her, touch her, suck on her breast. That was reserved for a man, Rose's husband, the husband who would take from her what she had shared with Rose for several months. She was glad now that she had waited as long as she had before asking the priest. She wished she had waited longer.

She knelt before the altar railing, leaning against

it, her head bowed. Reverently, she recited her penance.

Outside, Rose asked, "Well, love, are you pure again?" She had a mischievous grin on her face.

"Aye, and it's hard to be." While Rose stood on the sidewalk, Kathleen stopped on the first step. She looked Rose in the eye. "He said that we must stop what we are doing."

"You asked him about that?"

"I did. It's been on my mind, the right and the wrong of it. I was never sure, but now I am."

"Because some man wearing a black dress said so?" Rose's hands sliced the air before her as she spoke. The elevated train rattled above them.

"No! He knows by having studied hundreds of years of Catholic law," Kathleen answered. "That is, he knows women are to have children. It's our reason for being here."

Rose's lips went white and became thin, angry lines. "And by what authority does he speak for me?"

"He's a priest. He has the answers."

Rose started down the sidewalk. "He ain't me priest and he doesn't have me answers." She turned to Kathleen who was fighting to keep up with Rose's angry strides. "He's a man, that's all he is."

"He's a man of the cloth, Rose. You mustn't speak so of him."

Rose came up short, Kathleen nearly bumping into her. "All right, Kathleen. I won't. But I want you to know that this woman's body is not going to bear a dozen children by a husband I don't want. I don't want to be a mother. I don't want to be married. I want to be yours." Her voice became

184

pleading. "That's all I want, darling woman. Only to be yours." She grabbed Kathleen's hands. "Aren't you happy when you're in me arms?" she whispered.

Two men walked by and Kathleen waited before saying, "I am, Rose. You know I am, but I don't feel right about it. Not if I'm to marry."

"Why marry? Why do it if it's not what you want? Why, for God's sake?"

Kathleen brushed away persistent tears. She could not explain something this important to someone who was not Catholic. "It's just the way it is," she said. "There can be no other way."

"The hell there can't." Rose strode away from Kathleen.

"Rose, wait," Kathleen called. She hurried after her. "Wait," Kathleen said again. But Rose did not wait and was soon far ahead of Kathleen. It was obvious that Rose did not want Kathleen near her. She rounded a corner and was gone.

Kathleen turned back down Sixth Avenue, thinking she would walk through the park, to her apartment, the empty one, the one where, likely, Rose would not enter again. Her head down, her shoulders drooping, she passed St. Joseph's, refusing to bless herself, a habit she had picked up from others she had seen when they passed by the holy building.

She neared The Golden Swan at the southeast corner of Fourth Street, a raucous, darkly interiored pub where frequent fights took place. A weather-beaten sign with a faded image of a swan in flaking gold paint, creaked in the wind. The bar's large exterior window was filthy with age. Occasionally, strikers had marched with blackened eyes or broken

185

noses or hands from trying to prove a point or having one proved to them at the Hell-Hole, the more popular name for the bar.

Deep in thought, she barely had time to leap aside before a body came flying through the door and hit the sidewalk with a sickening thud at her feet. She watched, as if observing in slow motion, the woman's head strike the pavement. A man with thick arms and legs and a trunk as big around as an oil drum was upon the fallen lady, straddling her waist before she could rise.

"*No!*" Kathleen cried, and leaped at him as he firmly struck the woman. Without slowing his punches, he shook Kathleen off his back.

Kathleen attacked him again, and again he shook her loose. She picked herself up off the pavement, shouting for help, but no one was listening. This was too common an event, and unless someone was killed, she had long ago been told that the Swan was seldom disturbed.

"Stop that!" she cried. "Stop this instant, I tell you."

"Get away, bitch," he growled. "I'll hit her all I want. She's my wife!" Again, he swung at the prostrate woman.

By now several men and women had come out of the bar and were standing around, watching. Some laughed, some cursed, some cheered for the man, others for the woman.

"Let 'er have it, Dave," a man shouted drunkenly. "She's been asking for it all evening."

"No one asks for this," Kathleen screamed at the heckler.

"My wife does," a second man yelled. The small

crowd laughed at his comment while the man beating his wife hauled her up by her arm. She cried out in pain. Blood flowed freely from her nose.

Kathleen watched in confused horror as the woman's husband put a supporting arm around her waist and carefully helped her inside.

He looked back at Kathleen. Full of smug satisfaction, he said, "I love her, lady. Don't get me wrong. But she ain't gonna tell me what to do."

A woman thickly painted with rouge and powder laughed ridiculously. "He's right, honey. My old man used to do the same to me. I had it coming more than once. He was a good man, though. Strict as a school nun, he was. Stuck religiously to the rule o' thumb. Never switched me once with nothing bigger than his thumb, he didn't. A good man." Through rotting teeth, she continued laughing, following the crowd back inside.

Kathleen walked to the curb and vomited so violently she ruptured a blood vessel in her left eye. Only three months ago she had witnessed this same scene at this same bar. Only the husband and wife were different.

Often she had listened through the thin walls of her apartment, men and women screaming at each other or at their children in heated arguments. Sometimes the fights lasted throughout the night. She would wake feeling drugged from lack of sleep caused by the disputes.

She did not talk to Rose again. Except to go to work and to church, she holed up in her apartment. If Rose wanted to see her, she knew what time Kathleen usually attended mass. So far Rose had not shown up.

She wondered at the inconsistency of her life and that of the husbands who beat their wives and of the fighting going on around her in her own building. Why was that kind of hate and violence all right, yet what she felt for Rose so wrong?

"It can't be right," she said into the night. "I'm not wrong. I'm *not*."

CHAPTER SIXTEEN
Sunday, February 12, 1911

Yesterday, Kathleen had paid her rent. If not for the raise the strikers had won, she would never be able to afford living alone. As it was she ate sparingly in order to put aside a few cents each week in case of an emergency. She put a precious nickel in her pocket for collection at mass.

She arrived a little late and sat in the last pew, only half listening to the sermon. Looking over and around the tops of large-hatted women to Father

Michael, the two familiar ladies caught her eye. Always together, they were here each week receiving communion, and from time to time, Kathleen had seen them standing side by side waiting to go to confession. They were never with men, children or other women.

They sat to her right several pews ahead of her. The taller one had dark eyebrows, thin lips and an angular face. The smaller woman beside her had an aristocratic bearing, fair skin, blue eyes, blond silken hair. Both looked elegant and regal, richly dressed in warm tan and blue coats, the blond wearing feathers in her hat, the dark woman wearing a smaller hat tipped rakishly to one side. They sat with shoulders touching, unmoving, their eyes on the priest.

For the past several months, Kathleen had considered approaching them, asking them outright if they were in a romantic relationship. Each time she played the scene in her mind — how she would approach them, what she would ask — she froze with fear. If she were wrong, how ever would she explain herself?

But she was sure she was not wrong. Perhaps today she would ask them to clarify themselves. How, exactly, did they justify their love? She had been saying, "Perhaps today," for too long.

Father Michael's sermon faded to a distant monologue as she studied her hands, comparing one finger to another, their length, texture, size and the poor condition of the nails. Her knuckles had broadened from working so hard at the Triangle, the backs of her hands were square and roped with veins thick and raised. She studied them until there was nothing left in her mind except her two hands, one resting over the other, fingers motionless.

The women remained unmoving, their shoulders still in contact as if by accident and without conscious design. After all, many people sat shoulder to shoulder in the crowded pews. There was the man and woman just ahead of her, and the mother and her little boy right over there. And there were two ten-year-old girls. No one thought anything of it. It was crowded; shoulders touched. But, as she observed, no two women sat so close. Yes, those ladies sat like that on purpose. Touching. Shoulders touching. They always sat like that.

She wondered how long they had been in the relationship — a year at least, the length of time she and Rose had been apart, the length of time Rose had avoided looking at Kathleen, talking to her or acknowledging that Kathleen was even working in the same room with her. All the while Kathleen struggled with her questions, her doubts about her goodness, her evil side.

She could see how much the two women loved each other. All she wanted to know was how they managed to remain lovers and good Catholics too. The pull to speak to them was overpowering.

Father Michael's sermon ended. He was preparing for communion. One by one people filed forward, knelt at the altar, received Christ in the shape of a round, thin wafer on their tongues, prayed and swallowed the dry Host without allowing it to touch their teeth. They returned to their seats and knelt in quiet prayer, heads bowed, thoughts on Him.

She sat several rows behind the two women. How

could they receive Christ after having *touched* each other? How could they? They would go to hell. They would burn forever and ever.

And yet they did receive Communion, not mechanically, but reverently, and following them back, Kathleen watched them kneel in solemn prayer.

How? Kathleen questioned. These were two women. What priest had they gone to who would say to them their love was not wrong?

Mass ended with Kathleen compelled to follow the women out of the church. She was trembling fearfully when she finally made her way through the parishioners and caught up with them. She would not think at all, only act.

"I'm very sorry to intrude like this," she said. "I'm . . . I'm very, very sorry."

They both looked inquisitively at her.

"My name is Mary O'Daily," she lied. "I have a most personal question for you, and I think only you can answer it."

"Yes?" said the dark, handsome one.

"Forgive me," Kathleen said. She twisted her hands together, her panic mounting.

"How may we help you?" the blond lady asked.

A car pulled up along the curb. "Ready, misses?"

Their own automobile. Kathleen turned away, believing herself crazy for deciding to do this. Her knees became weak.

The handsome one held her arm, steadying her. "What's your question, dear?"

"It's very personal," Kathleen managed to say, forcing her words through a dry mouth.

"Yes?" The pretty one again.

"It's about what I think is happening between you two." Kathleen's voice was barely audible, her words choppy. "It's none of my business. None whatsoever."

The handsome one asked, "And what do you think is happening between us?"

"I've . . . I've watched over the weeks. I have a friend. I was in a . . . romantic . . . relationship. I don't know what God thinks of me. Father Michael says —"

"Join us in the auto," the dark one offered. "My name is Marcia." Nodding toward the blond lady, she said, "This is Sabine. Where do you live? We'll drive that way."

"Oh, I couldn't."

"It's best we don't stand on the sidewalk," Sabine said.

They put her between them, smiling at her, making her feel less frightened for her audaciousness.

When the car started forward, Marcia said, "The Lord wants people to love each other. That's why we're here, that and to help one another."

"But . . . what about confession? What does Father say?"

"We don't mention it," Sabine answered, smiling.

"But Father Michael said it's a sin."

Marcia laughed. "And that we are here only to have children. Yes, Father Michael said that to me years ago, and when I saw how unfair the rules seemed to be in real life, what he said no longer held meaning for me."

"We're not harming anyone," Sabine said.

"What about your souls?" Kathleen asked. Her heart raced as she listened.

Sabine primly folded her hands in her lap. "What about them? They're in no danger, at least no more so than that of some man beating his wife or giving her another child for the tenth time without regard to her feelings or that of the child's."

"Or he drinks until the early hours while his wife waits for him," Marcia said. "My father did that all his life. It finally killed my mother through sheer worry about where he was at night."

"Some time ago I watched a man beat his wife," Kathleen told them. "He said it was all right because she was his wife."

The car shifted as it rounded a corner. Sabine resettled herself. "He's wrong. Sinful, if you ask me."

"I wonder if he went to confession," Kathleen said.

"Or felt remorse if he isn't Catholic," added Marcia. "I'll say this about Protestants. They sure have it easy when they ask for forgiveness of sins."

"Sure, and it's true," Kathleen replied strongly. "Here I am."

The automobile pulled up to the curb before her tenement building. "I thank you for your time and your graciousness."

"You're quite welcome," said Marcia. "I expect we can rely on your discretion."

"Aye, you can." Kathleen waved to them as they drove off.

Upstairs, she sat at the table, her hands folded in front of her, carefully considering what she had just heard. An hour later, she was still there, unmoving. She rose and put on her coat. An O'Donald never gave up a good fight, and Kathleen considered herself as having been through quite a few of them in the past couple of years. She was well-seasoned like a good smoked ham.

At one thirty, she reached Rose's apartment, teeth clenched, her mind filled with determination.

Rose had just come in from a lively walk. Her cheeks were pink, her hair slightly windblown. She opened the door, surprise registering on her face.

Kathleen blurted, "I was wrong about any danger to my soul."

"Come on," Rose said, glancing back at her roommates and snatching up her coat. They left for the outside and away from the others.

They strolled unspeaking for several blocks, Kathleen's chest bloated with fear. She should not have barged in on Rose. It was good of her to walk with Kathleen.

Rose asked, "What changed your mind?"

Kathleen attempted to wet her lips with a dry tongue. She played with a button in her pocket, turning it over and over between nervous fingers. Taking a deep breath, she plunged in. "A couple of things," she said. "This morning I talked with two women who go to my church. They're in a romantic relationship, but they still go to confession and communion. They told me they don't talk about their relationship to Father Michael. They don't believe he needs to know."

"Why should they?" Rose asked. From her coat pocket, she pulled out frayed gloves with missing fingers and pulled them on. "Husbands and wives don't confess their romantic relationship, do they?"

"They're married."

"Maybe those two women consider themselves married."

"I don't understand how that's possible, but you might be right."

"I am right," Rose answered, not giving an inch. "To be married doesn't take a preacher saying words over two people. It takes two people saying words over themselves. If they believe they're married, then they're married. The trick is not to move on once you've made such a decision, but to stay and stick it out for better or worse, for richer or poorer and in sickness or health. We have an advantage though. We don't have to obey anybody. I'd honor me darling, though." Rose smiled softly.

"You believe just saying the words to each other makes you married?" Kathleen stopped and looked open-mouthed at Rose. "That's heresy."

"If each of you means it, I do. You said there was something else that made you think you were right."

"It was aboard ship," Kathleen said as they began walking again. "The loss of the loved ones that were buried at sea — I felt like I was the one who had lost someone." She tucked her hands into her pockets. "I've been thinking about how bad it is to lose someone you love. It's bad, to be sure. I lost my parents. And then I foolishly lost you." The unspoken question hung in the air: Have I lost you?

Rose watched her, studied her. "No, love, you never lost me. Not for a moment. I've seen no one the way I saw you. I haven't wanted anyone the way I want you. I want you like a man would want a wife, only I don't want to be a man, and I don't

196

want you waiting on me like you're a wife."
Abstractedly, she studied the buildings. "I can't
explain it exactly."

They walked to the park to where they had
attended so many secret union meetings in the dark.
There were several swings toward their left.
Childlike, they ran over to them, each claiming a
swing and pumping her feet until she was parallel
with the cross bar from which the swings hung.
They threw back their heads and laughed like wee
ones and challenged each other as to who could fly
the highest.

Children came over to stand waiting until the
grownups gave up their seats and moved off.

Kathleen fixed her gaze upon Rose. Without
preamble, she said, "Will you marry me, Rose?"

Something came up behind Rose's eyes and a
smile crossed her lips. "You've changed your
thinking, then?"

"Aye, I have, but I still consider myself a good
girl."

"The good Lord never doubted that, lass, nor did
I."

"Then will you marry me?" Kathleen's eyes shone
like morning stars. She was afraid, she was always
afraid, but somehow she made it through everything.
She would survive a no from Rose if she had to.

"When?"

"Now." She folded her fingers into her palms and
dug in deep.

"Now?" Rose echoed. Her voice was like a warm
embrace in the cool air.

"I know the words that you said earlier. We
could say them."

"I have no ring to give you."

"We don't need rings. I only want to love you."

Rose moved to Kathleen's side. "I'll marry you," she said, taking Kathleen's hand in her own. "I'll marry you for better or for worse, in sickness and in health, whether you're rich or poor. And I'll always honor and cherish you, Kathleen. Always." She looked at Kathleen with something very strong in her eyes.

Kathleen straightened her back and repeated Rose's words.

"I'll kiss you tonight, Kathleen, darling. I'll lie on top of you, head to toe. I'll tuck your head beneath me chin and hook me feet beneath yours. Me arms will be wrapped around you, and one hand will cradle your head against me. I'll love you forever, Kathleen, forever and ever."

A powerful exultation filled Kathleen's heart. She had to breathe deeply several times to steady herself.

They held hands as though friends, understanding that their touch gave a promise of a night of passion and caring and commitment.

They returned to Rose's building to gather her things. "I haven't got much," Rose said.

Kathleen smiled. "Who does?"

Her friends wished her well, saying they did not blame her for moving. They would find another girl to take her place, and Rose would be a big help to poor Kathleen who still lived alone.

They laughed all the way there, carrying Rose's possessions in several bags, being careful to watch their step at the curbs since they could not see over their bags.

After settling in, they prepared a frugal supper. They ate hurriedly.

Kathleen felt as light as a feather, and later, lying nude beneath Rose, wrapped in her arms and Rose's weight resting on her, she sighed with relief. This is where she was supposed to be. Rose would be her romantic relationship for the rest of their lives.

Rose pressed her pelvis against Kathleen's. Kathleen opened her legs, allowing Rose to nestle between them. For a while, they moved in rhythm, fitting together, the heat from their bodies rising, their breathing steadily increasing.

"I want to do something, Rose."

"What?" Rose murmured in her ear.

"I want to touch you and to watch it happen."

Rose raised up on one elbow. "Surely you're not serious."

"Aye, I am. You're beautiful. I'd like to see you."

"I never heard of such a thing. And you such a fine Catholic lady."

"I am, but I'm also yours for life. That, and knowing that loving you is right for me, makes me want to see you, to know all of you. What's wrong with that?"

"I can't imagine it."

"I can. It makes me want to swallow you whole."

"Well . . ."

"I'll get the lamp."

"You don't need any lamp."

"I need the lamp. I want to see properly."

Rose shook her head. "Aye, and you've always been a proper one, haven't you? And don't you think there's light enough?"

"No, I'd only see shadows. You're more than a shadow."

Rose said no more as Kathleen jumped up. She lighted the lamp turning the wick on high, then placed it on a chair at the foot of the bed.

"Are you sure you can see all right, now?" Rose asked, sounding slightly irritated.

"Sure, and you'll be lovely." Kathleen ran a hand from Rose's foot to her throat. "You are lovely, Rose. And how is it you're so shy?"

"I've never been studied right *there* before."

"I don't believe you," Kathleen said. Rose began to pull up the blankets Kathleen had cast aside when she had gone for the lantern, but Kathleen drew them back.

"Kathleen, it's not like it's summertime in this room. I'm freezing."

"I won't keep you uncovered for long, Rose darling. Just let me look for a moment. You can close your eyes."

"Be sure that I will."

Her body was soft and radiant. With tender firmness, Kathleen moved Rose's knees apart and sat between them. She put a palm against Rose's mound. Rose moaned, and Kathleen saw her frown slightly. "Did I hurt you?"

Rose released a satisfied sound as Kathleen moved her palm in a circular motion. Rose opened her legs farther. Using both hands, Kathleen separated Rose's outer soft lips and then her thin, pink inner lips.

"Heavens, we're complicated," Kathleen whispered. "You are so beautiful." She moved a finger over the rise in stiffened flesh she saw there. Rose's skin glistened with moisture.

Kathleen gazed upon Rose with delightful wonder, Rose looking much like the undulating hills of her native Ireland. "You look creamy," Kathleen said. "Good enough to eat."

"Do it." Rose's voice sounded far away. Kathleen was pleased to see Rose looking at her and reaching toward her with both hands. She put her palms against Kathleen's face and drew her down. "I want you to touch me with your tongue."

"My tongue?"

"You're not timid, are you?" Rose eyes were molten pools of lead. "Because I'm not. Not anymore. You make me want you like that, with your tongue." She closed her eyes and tugged purposefully on Kathleen's face.

Kathleen bent to meet Rose's body, reveling in this new act.

Rose was tangy, almost salty. The touch of her against Kathleen's mouth caused Kathleen's groin to spasm. She pressed harder, her head moving slowly, rhythmically, her tongue darting against yielding heights and depths.

Rose held Kathleen's head in place, moved her hips from side to side, up and down. She moaned, quietly at first, then more loudly and more rapidly.

Kathleen had been kneeling over Rose. Now she stretched out fully, kicking aside the blankets inhibiting her feet. She felt the mattress against her pelvis and pressed just as she pressed against Rose. As Rose built with more and more heat, Kathleen did the same. It was hard to remain where she was and not leap upon Rose and grind her hips against Rose's own. It was hard to think only of Rose and not of this lava between her own legs. She forced her mind away from herself and back to the fire beneath her tongue.

Rose thrashed about, her body arching high and then falling back to the bed. She's wild, Kathleen thought, staying coupled with her, not letting her go.

Rose let out a shriek and still Kathleen stayed. Rose pulled on Kathleen's face and after the third attempt, freed herself. "I . . . I can't stand anymore, darling. No more." She yanked Kathleen to her, not at all gently. "Ah, darling, darling, darling." She began to sob, trembling in Kathleen's arms. Teardrops moistened cheeks.

Kathleen asked, "Why do you cry?"

Rose said, "For the same reason I laugh. It's high time I threw aside the covers." She turned her head and talked into Kathleen's hair. "I don't know why you're not bashful. But you're not. I can learn things from you. Loving things. I hope you love me like that again — with the lamp on." She smiled.

Kathleen raised up on an elbow. "Take me where you were."

"With all the love in the world," Rose whispered, her lips moving against Kathleen's forehead.

She rolled over onto Kathleen, cupping Kathleen's body against her own, burying her lover beneath her.

"I like to have you lay on top of me," Kathleen said. Rose's hair covered her face, and Kathleen nibbled on strands of it. "I feel so loved then. Wanted."

"You are wanted, darling Kathleen. More than you know."

She moved down between Kathleen's legs, her longer body extending beyond the end of the bed. "I've thought about doing this to you a million different times," Rose said in a husky voice. Her hands were on Kathleen's nipples, her tongue darting between Kathleen's lips.

Kathleen watched Rose's mouth moving against her, her hair framing Rose's lips. Rose's eyes were closed in ecstasy as she cupped Kathleen's breasts, her hips pressing against the bed as Kathleen's had done.

Without conscious control, Kathleen felt her knees bend and her legs fold against her body. She listened to Rose's heavy breathing, felt her hot breath against her own cooler skin. She shivered in anticipation of the supreme moment she knew she would experience. She was already almost there.

When it hit her, she was no longer sure she was still on the bed. She might be near the ceiling or possibly the moon, with nothing but space beneath her. She grunted like a rutting animal and then cried. She had closed her eyes when she knew she was near. Now she opened them, not recognizing the ceiling above her. She was completely detached and disoriented. The ceiling looked crooked, or perhaps she imagined it. The sensation frightened her, and she reached over to grip the edge of a chair alongside the bed. She needed to anchor herself to something other than this floating bed where she lay.

She tugged at Rose's head until Rose moved up beside her, holding her, swallowing her with her body. She repeated Rose's name over and over, thoughts of Rose's lips still upon her. She felt herself dripping with wetness, felt it seep beneath her buttocks. Tears seared her eyes and cheeks. She cried hard against Rose's chest.

"Are you all right, Kathleen darling?"

Kathleen's tears continued falling and then she began to laugh. "Aye, I'm all right. I'm as all right as I could ever be, beloved Rose. You make me all right. You make everything in the world all right. Aye, my love. I'm all right, and I always will be with you by my side."

They fell asleep rolled up in each other's arms.

CHAPTER SEVENTEEN

Saturday, March 25, 1911

Lovemaking between Kathleen and Rose had been
reduced to weekends, and even then, they were often
too tired from their jobs. But life was better
otherwise. They had their privacy, their simple meals
with just the two of them. Kathleen did not have to
struggle so to pay her rent. Once in a while, they
took in a moving picture show. Recently, Rose had
bought a new hat with a large red flower on it for
forty-five cents. She loved it dearly and sometimes

when she cooked supper, she wore it just for the pure pleasure the hat gave her. And in spite of the snow still lying thick on the ground and rooftops of the city, the March winds seemed warmer. These days the sun against the bricks of the buildings, made the streets seem a bit more cozy.

Things were going well until this morning when, for the first time since hitting America's shores, Kathleen woke up sick — too sick, she thought, to go to work.

She worried herself into a frenzy until Rose said, "I'll go to work. You stay and rest. You'd rest if I was a husband telling you to. So do it!"

And Kathleen did, vastly relieved that Rose had put her illness in perspective. Rose was right. A proper husband would have had his wife stay in bed.

"Come to work if you feel better," Rose said just before leaving. "I'll tell Dobbs you might be in later."

Kathleen rolled over, gripping her sides. "I'll bet it was the fish we had last night. I don't like fish."

"You eat it every Friday," Rose reminded her.

"I hate it every Friday."

"Then why do you eat it?"

"Catholic law — and habit, I guess."

"Then we'll switch to rabbit or chicken."

"No, no meat. Not on Friday."

Rose rolled her eyes. "All right. You skip eating fish on Friday and fill up on potatoes or rice. We'll think of something." She leaned over and kissed Kathleen on the nose. "Maybe I'll see you later."

Kathleen slept most of the day. She woke feeling groggy but better. Near quitting time, she would meet Rose and walk her home. She rose and dressed.

She reached Washington Place by four-thirty, and it was then she saw the first puff of smoke issuing from the Asch Building's upper floors. She blinked several times, the shock of the smoke staggering her. Fire? God in Heaven, she prayed, don't let that be a fire up there. No one'll make it out alive.

Backing down Greene Street for a better look, she saw the first bundle of clothing tossed from the eighth story window. She was outraged that cloth had more value to the Triangle than its workers. Then she realized how wrong she had been. It was not a cloth bundle that fell. It was a woman. She hit the sidewalk with a thud. Not just a thud, but a sickening dull thunk.

Already, dozens of women's faces were framed in the windows that had finally been opened, the flames roaring, licking fingers of death leaping at them. Several onlookers had stopped on the street. Others were running toward the fire. Kathleen too, ran closer, scanning the faces, searching desperately for her beloved Rose.

Her stomach muscles twisted into a screaming, searing pain making her fall to her knees. Those women were going to fall — or deliberately jump — eighty feet to their deaths. They would die in a desperate attempt to save themselves and only land with —

THUD!

"Rooooose!" she screamed. But no one listened to a live woman screeching healthily on her knees. They listened, as she did, to another thud and then another and another.

In a brief span of time, dozens of people, and quickly, hundreds, had gathered. Voices from everywhere were shrieking, "Call the firemen. Get a ladder." Men frantically ran back and forth trying to keep the crowd from pressing toward the building. People cried out, "Don't jump! Don't jump!" but then another one would. From Broadway to the park, it seemed, thousands of people had lined the streets.

Kathleen slid to one side and was out cold. She came to in seconds as a man hauled her upright. He fanned her with his hat. "You all right, lady? You all right?"

She nodded yes, and he left her instantly to run to a fallen victim. She watched with horror as the next dozen bodies dressed in coats and hats, obviously ready to leave the building for the day, fell, hit, and died. Ah, God, Kathleen's heart cried out, why couldn't You have waited just five more minutes for this fire to begin?

And where was Rose? *WHERE WAS ROSE?*

Kathleen could picture the fire raging inside, the shirtwaists hanging above the girls' heads and going up like crepe paper, the collection bins at their feet, spontaneous infernos, the tables so close together that no one could move fast. And she already knew that one of the freight elevators was not working.

Then she remembered something else. She broke through the police barrier ringing the building and ran to the Greene Street door.

"Are you nuts, lady? Get the hell away from here!" A huge man in police uniform guarded the door against those fighting to get in while directing those still able to make it down the stairs, telling them to run to safety. Brutally, he shoved her aside.

"But the fire door is sealed," she shouted at him. "Someone has to go up and open it."

"Can't nobody get close to open it, lady," he said. "It's too damn hot up there."

Others were screaming at him in multiple languages and nearly crushing him as he pushed and they pushed, and he, trying to protect everyone, won by sheer determination alone.

"They'll die," she screamed at him as she scrambled away. "They'll die, they'll die."

He ignored her as he helped those he could.

The firemen had arrived as bodies continued falling like rain. Fire ladders were thrown up, but were useless. They did not reach the eighth floor.

Kathleen ducked beneath the barrier and ran to the west side of the building. In the rear courtyard the only fire escape existed. With the fire door sealed, people from the upper three burning floors were rapidly spilling out through windows onto it. The fire escape began at the roof of the building with an eighteen-inch ladder leading down to a small landing at each floor and then more stairs before ending abruptly at the second floor. From there was a drop ladder thirteen feet long suspended above a glass skylight of a ground-floor extension pushed out into the yard. The escape was quickly crammed with people trapped at the eighth floor by heavy sheet-iron shutters opened outward, buckled and frozen in place by the heat of the fire. Kathleen searched the workers' distorted, panicky faces. She did not see Rose.

Behind the barrier again, she watched a woman from the ninth floor wave her arms, fighting to keep her body upright as she fell. When she hit, she folded like an accordion. And there was that persistent *thud* everyone heard. Bodies lay scattered with nothing left to the corpses except heaps of clothing, twisted limbs and broken bones.

Several firemen ran to the foot of a window with a life net. As they did, two more women jumped. The men got the net positioned in time, and the women sailed right through it and died. Before the net could be moved, another woman landed on top of the first two.

Transfixed, hundreds watched as body after body jumped, hit and made that awful sound. Kathleen could not even think of those burning alive inside, only of those she could see.

She watched as a young man in a hat helped a woman to a window sill. He carefully held her out and then let her drop. He held out two more women the same way, helping them die, helping them to be brave.

Another woman came to the window. She put her arms around the man and kissed him. Mr. Jamison and Minna!

"No," Kathleen screamed. She held out a hand, futilely reaching for them. *"No!"*

Jamison then held Minna as he had the others. She fell from his arms to her death. Without pause, he leaped to the windowsill. His coat flapped behind him as he came down. Air filled his trousers legs. In less time than it took Kathleen to gasp, he lay in a tattered heap on the pavement among the women who had fallen before him.

At another window, women fought one another, their hair and clothing aflame. They fought until they were forced to jump. Kathleen dully wondered if they were fighting to be the first to die. She watched Bertha, whose hands could have conducted a great orchestra, jump, and then Ursula whom she had once sat next to. Only the day before she had told Kathleen of becoming a grandmother for the first time. Then Betty jumped, only fourteen years old and the youngest girl on Kathleen's floor. From the ninth floor came Abigale who once had wanted only what she believed was right for Kathleen and Rose, and who, within seconds, would learn if she had been correct or not. Kathleen prayed for their souls.

And the thuds continued from the eighth, ninth and tenth floors.

Without warning a great, wrenching sound of metal filled the air. Kathleen knew without seeing, the fire escape was collapsing beneath the weight of bodies on it. She was aware that more people were falling and dying, crashing through the skylight to the room below.

From her position on the southeast corner of Greene and Washington across from the building, Kathleen, now in shock, listened and stared in horror, her eyes unblinking, watching, watching, watching the windows for Rose.

And then Rose came. She stood looking out of the window as if she were viewing a beautiful vista before her, clouds of smoke pouring out on either side of her. She had on her coat, smoldering now, perhaps with some perverse thought that the coat would break her fall. She loved that coat. It was nearly a rag, but she was attached to it.

Kathleen began to whimper, her eyes swimming in tears, her breath caught in her throat. Rose climbed to the sill and without pause, leaped. She landed with a thud, that godawful thud that filled the air. She landed on several other bodies. The coat did not help break her fall at all. Kathleen fainted.

She came to on a pew in St. Joseph's. As from a dream she came to screaming. Hers were not the only screams. The church walls echoed hysterical screams, incoherent screams, screams that made no sense, screams in languages Kathleen did not recognize, screams that ripped open the seams of her heart and left it bare and ripe for the loss, of loneliness, of hell.

She sat up, dazed. A nun came to her side. "What's your name, dear?"

Kathleen did not answer, and the nun spoke in Yiddish, German, Italian and then in English again before Kathleen understood what she was saying.

Several seconds passed before she could remember who she was. "I . . . I'm Kathleen O'Donald." And then she remembered the fire — and Rose. Rose had jumped, and Kathleen started screaming all over again, seeing Rose climb onto the sill and leap into the air. She screamed and screamed and screamed.

She came to again, still lying on the pew. This time when she sat up no one helped her. She did not scream either. She would not scream again. She would not live again. Her parents' deaths, the burials at sea, and Rose's fall shot through her mind. She leaned on the back of the pew ahead of her, cradled her head in her arms and wept.

It was dark and very late when she left the church and headed toward Ellie's place. Digging into her pocket she found a dime.

Sitting alone at a table, she sipped tea without tasting it. She should go back to the apartment, but the very thought of Rose's things there . . . Without Rose, there was nothing — *NOTHING!* She pushed aside the tea and rested her head in her arms.

"Kathleen?" Someone slid into the booth across from her. Kareen! That her life had been spared took a moment to register. "I saw you come in," Kareen said.

The place was filling up, people spontaneously gathering at this popular spot of the workers. The talk was only about the fire, the dead, the sealed fire escape that people somehow still managed to crawl out onto and what was to be done.

"The air shaft in the rear of the building had a heap of dead girls at the bottom of it," a man whispered, his eyes haunted.

"I saw the water," said another. "It weren't water at all. It were blood, only blood." He sat heavily in a chair and stared into space. "And the policeman went about with tags with numbers on 'em and put 'em on the dead folks."

"Officer O'Clancy said there's fifty bodies in the big room on the ninth floor. They didn't make it out."

Rose made it out. Rose jumped.

"I struck for better conditions," Kathleen said. She spoke in a whisper, but people were still and listened. "I wanted it cleaner in there and safer. Those bins under our machines? Nothing but trouble looking for a problem." She looked up at those who had gathered around her. "Rose is dead, you know. I loved her." Her eyes were big pools of terror, incomprehensible visions still floating through her mind.

"We all lost somebody," a man sobbed. He hung his head, unable to speak further.

"Did you go to the morgue and see if it's really her?" somebody asked.

"Morgue?" she asked dully.

"They's keeping the dead down by the police station. You could go there and see."

The thought of looking through rows of dead bodies filled Kathleen with stark terror. She began to rise. A hand on her shoulder steadied her.

"Maybe she ain't dead. Maybe you didn't see her."

"I watched her go."

Oh, yes, Rose was dead all right. Even with landing on other bodies, the force of her fall pushed them all through that fancy, thick glass sidewalk.

"Why'nt you go home, dear?" an elderly woman suggested.

"Why don't you all go home?" Ellie said. Small, round and robust, she pulled out several coffee cups from beneath the counter and placed them on top. "Have a cup of coffee on me, and then go home." She put her pudgy hand on the man nearest her, her eyes tearful. "I lost a lot of customers today, all of 'em friends. There just ain't no use of sitting and crying all night long. You got families that need you right now. They'll be looking for you. Have some coffee and then go on home."

They did as she suggested and in an hour's time, the place was empty.

214

Kathleen left with the last of them, two men whom she did not know seeing her safely home. With leaden feet she started up the stairs.

Grace popped her head out and lumbered toward Kathleen. "You're alive! Thank the good Lord!" Grace grabbed her in a great embrace. "I heard a hundred people died in the Triangle." She stepped back and repeatedly blessed herself.

"Sure, and it had to be more than that," Kathleen managed to say.

"Where's Rose?" Grace asked, but by then Kathleen was halfway up the stairs, and she was not listening anyway.

She put her key into the lock, dreading the thought of going inside. In her mind's eye she could already see Rose's clothes strung here and there, a habit Kathleen had not been able to change in her, and her makeup on the dresser, a towel draped over the chair drying from this morning's face-washing.

She walked in, leaving the door ajar. The hallway lamp shed weak shadows across the floor and into the room. She sat at the table and took the towel from the back of the chair. She buried her face in it and drank in Rose's smell.

A voice whispered from the bed, "Oh, me God, oh, me dear God in heaven above."

Kathleen's entire body felt as if it had gone to sleep, tingling as though a jolt of lightning had touched every nerve. A figure slowly rose from the bed. An apparition! Kathleen got up from the chair and backed away from the thing coming at her, floating toward her, its arms outstretched, threatening her. She heard a scream from somewhere, felt the floor go out from beneath her feet. The devil had come for her.

She was lying on the bed when she came to. "And that's why I think you're mixed up," the woman said to her.

She saw without comprehending. This woman looked just like Rose had looked — before Rose hit the sidewalk, before Rose went — *thud!*

"You're very kind," Kathleen said. "You're very kind."

She slept in the woman's arms that night. The next day she sat across the table from her. The woman helped her eat warm soup and kept saying something to her about a coat. She could not quite understand what was being told to her, but she answered politely. She spent all her time staring at the window, watching Rose fall through the air, her coat wrapped tightly around her as if hoping it would break her fall. And of course it did not help her at all. Rose still went thud.

"Thud," Kathleen said. "Thud."

"What did you say?" the apparition asked.

"Thud," Kathleen answered. "Rose went thud when she hit. They all went thud. Thud, thud, thud, thud . . ."

"Don't keep saying that, Kathleen. Don't keep thinking about it. It's over. I'm safe. Look at me." She forced Kathleen to look at her.

"Thud," Kathleen said. "Thud, thud, thud . . ." She began to scream the word, repeating it over and over. She clamped her hands over her ears and squeezed her eyes shut. "Thud," she screamed. She thought she would never stop screaming.

"Goddamn it, Rose! What are you doing?" Kathleen could feel the slaps landing over and over. "Stop it, stop, I say."

Rose stopped.

Kathleen blinked herself back to near reality. "Rose? Rose? Rose? Rose?"

Rose hit her again.

Weeping hysterically, Kathleen fell against her saying, "But your coat. I saw you jump. But your coat. I saw you jump."

"It wasn't me, darling. It was poor Mrs. Jenkens. I gave her me coat. I gave it away yesterday morning."

Kathleen stared blankly at her. "You gave away your coat?"

Rose nodded.

"*You gave away your coat?*"

"Aye. It was warm enough yesterday to wear just the old ragged one that ain't much use. I gave it away. I still have that one there." She pointed to a coat in somewhat better condition, hanging from a hook on the door.

"You gave away your coat?" Kathleen did not believe her.

"She needed a coat. I had two."

"*I thought you jumped. Goddamn you. I thought you jumped.*" Kathleen fell upon Rose's chest, beating her fists against her. "I thought it was you. I lost you. I believed I'd lost you."

Rose grasped her wrists, holding them until her rage subsided. She fell against Rose. "Never, darling Kathleen. Never." She held Kathleen's tear-drenched face between her hands. "It was only me coat. I wasn't even there. I got sick too, and ran to the toilet room to throw up. The fire started right after that. It spread all over the place in minutes. Several of us ran downstairs right then. We came out on Washington."

Tears welled up in Kathleen's eyes. "But where were you? I never saw you."

"I couldn't get through the crowd. Then the policemen were stopping everybody trying to get names. I couldn't get away from them. You must have been in the crowd too. I came home hoping you hadn't gone to work. But it looked like you had and I ran back. I watched for you, but I didn't see you jump."

Kathleen's stomach heaved.

"I looked in the police morgue for you and at St. Joseph's. I don't know how I missed you. I didn't know if you were dead or alive. I had no way of knowing since you weren't at the morgue. So I came home and waited, hoping and praying. I didn't hear you come in. I can't believe I slept. Goddamn me. Goddamn me!" She clutched Kathleen to her. "You're safe, me darling. You're safe. I'll never let you go. Not ever!"

They cried in each other's arms all night long and all the next day. They cried for dead friends, for those who would never love their boyfriends or their girlfriends or their husbands or wives. They cried for the unnecessary deaths and the orphans the fire created.

They cried for each other.

CHAPTER EIGHTEEN

Tuesday, March 28, 1911

Three days after the fire the Triangle Shirtwaist Company put a notice in the trade papers that they were opened again. They had installed themselves at University Place. The union, not to be kept in the dark about management's movement even though the annual contract had been signed in good conscience, found that the company had again already blocked the exit to the single fire escape by two rows of sewing machines. They had not learned a thing.

While the company was making sure it could produce maximum quota, a three-mile-long mourning procession with various union factions carrying the banners of their trade, moved through Manhattan's streets.

The police did not bother the thousands and thousands of men and women who marched for the one hundred and thirty-three women and thirteen men killed in a fire that lasted half an hour. There were no carriages, no mounted police, just the mourners in a line that went on for miles and for hours.

In the middle of the group walked Kathleen and Rose. They shed tears with the rest; they mourned with the rest; they raged with the rest. They asked the same question others asked: "What can we do so this will not happen again?"

On April second, there was a memorial meeting held in the Metropolitan Opera House. Kathleen and Rose and hundreds of others packed the place to listen to Rabbi Wise.

"Why," he asked, "when this tragedy was preventable, was it not prevented?"

Kathleen listened in respectful silence while fury screamed through her mind. The crowd murmured low when the rabbi questioned the laws that allowed such genocide of workers, and then shouted when he talked of going before the New York State legislature with demands for reform.

They cheered him, tears streaming down their cheeks, when he told them that while property is good, life is better; and that while possessions are valuable, life is priceless; that individuals were more than pieces of machinery; that those responsible would be judged by Someone higher than themselves.

Rose Schneiderman, organizer for the International Ladies' Garment Workers' Union and the Women's Trade Union League, spoke of the thousands of women maimed on the job, the terrible truth that there were so many workers available for just one job that it mattered little to management if one hundred and forty-six were burned to death. She told the spellbound audience that every time workers struck — in the only way they knew to protest deplorable working conditions — the law allowed attacks against the strikers in a sometimes vicious and brutal manner. The worker was beaten back when he rose and was forced to continue living and working in unbearable situations.

Schneiderman said, "I will not talk fellowship to you gathered before me; not with all the blood that had been shed. It is for you yourselves, the working people, to save yourselves. What you need is a strong working-class movement."

The house came down with a roar. They believed her; they believed in her. She was right; Rabbi Wise was right; the union was right! There was thunderous applause when they stood. They reached out and held hands and raised their clasped hands high. Audience members joined hands and raised them in solidarity with Schneiderman and Wise. Kathleen felt at one with them — they were one! They would continue to fight whatever was wrong with the hellish sweatshop system.

The meeting over, the crowd filed out, talking of grief, lost spouses, lost friends.

"I wonder how many lost a romantic lover," Kathleen said. She pulled her coat tighter.

"I know of four different couples, and of the —" Rose paused and swallowed hard. "You and I are the only couple left."

Kathleen stumbled at hearing Rose's words. She thought she was going to faint like she did at the fire. "*Thud, thud, thud.*"

Rose grabbed her before she fell and held her close. They moved off to one side, away from the questioning eyes of the passersby. "Tip your head back, darling. Breathe deep. We're all right. We're both here. See? Look at me. I'm fine. You're fine. We're all right."

Kathleen gulped in big breaths of air, fighting the sounds and sights of the fire, bodies landing, sirens screeching, people hysterically crying, tearing their hair, wrenching their clothing. She could smell burning flesh and see the men and women crowded at the windows. She could see them falling one at a time, *thud* against the cement, some folding like Chinese fans, others splatting as their heads hit and split like melons. *Thud.*

She started to black out, and felt the slap of Rose's hand. "Pull yourself together, Kathleen. Snap out of this. I'm all right, I tell you."

Kathleen came back to herself. "It's not only you. It's all of them. All those people, dead because of money, because a shirtwaist meant more than the life of a human being. Are we nothing but dispensable pieces of machinery? Is that all we are?" She sobbed wildly against Rose.

Rose cradled Kathleen's head. "No, and we'll not

allow ourselves to be less than we are. We'll fight, that's what we'll do."

"Fight," Kathleen said weakly. "I don't know if I can fight anymore. I just don't know."

The following morning they went back to work at the Triangle Shirtwaist Company, now located on the ninth floor at University Place.

CHAPTER NINETEEN
Wednesday, December 27, 1911

Because they were barred from entering the courtroom, the dead victims' families and friends packed the street outside and the corridors within. After a three-week trial, a verdict was anticipated sometime today.

Kathleen and Rose had skipped work this morning, as had several hundred others, to hear the jury's decision firsthand. She and Rose had gotten up at three A.M. to be sure that as soon as the building opened they would be at least one of the first to strategically stand by the courtroom door.

It wasn't long before she was crammed against the wall next to the doors. The crush of people against her caused her to feel ill and claustrophobic. Rose, fighting to stay by her side, was so close that Kathleen could feel her breath against her cheek. The slight sensation comforted her.

Kathleen watched the accused owners enter and listened to the crowd shrieking, "Murderers! Murderers! Make them suffer for killing our children." The names of the dead, spoken in several tongues, rose shrilly above the deeper wailing of the bereaved. It was a daily occurrence, each time the crowd caught a glimpse of the Triangle's owners, the men who had escaped the fire by climbing onto the roof.

They were charged with the crime of manslaughter of Margaret Schwartz, in its first and second degrees.

When learning of the charges weeks before, Kathleen had been stunned. "And no one else? What of the other one hundred, forty-five?"

Rose, as dumbstruck as Kathleen, could not even respond.

Kathleen, along with two men, had her ear pressed tightly against the courtroom's double doors. Once in a while, she or one of the men would peek through the crack and report in a whisper, what was happening. The news was relayed like lightning.

Peering inside, Kathleen watched District Attorney Bostwick closely question a tearful little girl also named Rose, who had witnessed the deadly fire. She was clear and precise, never missing a beat in her explanation. Then the District Attorney turned his witness over to Max D. Steuer, defending attorney of Harris and Blanck.

He, too, spoke gently to the girl, not badgering her, not encouraging her to say something she would not otherwise be expected to say. Instead, he spent a half hour in finding out whom she had seen, where she lived, who took care of her and where she had been since the fire.

Then Steuer said, "Now, Rose, in your own words and in your own way, please tell the jury everything that you did and said and everything you saw from when you first saw the flames." He used precisely the same words District Attorney Bostwick had used.

Kathleen took a moment to loosen a cramp setting in at the base of her neck. She turned her attention back to the tiny opening.

With the exception of a single word, Rose repeated the story she had told Bostwick.

Then Steuer asked, "Didn't you leave out a word when you answered this question before?"

"Did I?" she said.

He answered, "I think you did." He asked her other things at that point, unrelated to the fire, and half an hour later again repeated his question to her. "Now, Rose, in your own words and in your own way, please tell the jury everything that you did, and said, and everything you saw from when you first saw the flames."

So Rose repeated the answer, and when she came to the missing word she said, "Oh, yes," and put in the word, identically reciting her answer.

Throughout the trial, Kathleen and the two men carefully relayed information as accurately as possible.

"She's been coached," Rose whispered to Kathleen.

"By who?"

"I don't know. The D.A., Steuer. Maybe both. We're in trouble."

Kathleen yielded her position to Rose. "You listen. My neck's broken."

A second witness was put through much the same type of questioning. According to Rose, she, too, sounded coached.

There were closing arguments, and at 4:45 P.M., three weeks after the trial had begun, the jury returned with their verdict. Deliberations had taken only one hour and fifty minutes.

Kathleen and Rose had long since moved toward the back of the crowd. In the corridor a man shouted, "The verdict's in. Isaac and Blanck are acquitted!"

The defendants were quickly escorted to the anteroom. They tried to avoid the waiting crowd but were spotted in a far corridor. Men, women and children cried out, "Give me back my daughter, my son, my husband, brother, sister." A man broke by Kathleen and through the wild group. He shook his fist in the owners' faces, crying, "Not guilty? Not guilty? It was murder! Murder!" Still screaming, he collapsed at their feet.

"I've got to get out of here," Rose said, literally dragging Kathleen by her arm. They fought their way through the hysterical mob and emerged on the front step of the courthouse. They breathed deeply of the easy wind blowing by, the snowflakes slowly drifting down.

"Those lives," Kathleen said. "Those precious lives dumped into the water like so much fish bait."

Rose drew her collar up around her throat. She grabbed her hat as a gust of wind bent back the brim. "What are you talking about?"

"Aboard ship," Kathleen said, stuffing her mittened hands into the large deep pocket of her black wool coat. "With hardly any time spent at all on the fact that those people would never be seen again, they were dumped overboard. And that's what happened to the women and men who died in the fire. They were here, and now they're gone. It's like life doesn't mean anything. Anything at all."

Rose put a bold arm around Kathleen's shoulders. "We do mean something, Kathleen. We're not just pieces of meat like cows and horses and chickens. We have purpose and we have a life to offer. A good life."

"You sound like Father Michael."

"I sound like an important person, important just because I'm a human being. And you're important too. And so were the dead buried at sea and the dead we buried from the fire." She gripped Kathleen tighter. "We're all important."

"Not all, some people are a waste."

Rose thought that over. "Yes, I suppose some are. Indeed, they are."

They walked down the steps. Rose took Kathleen by the arm as a man might a woman.

Tiredly, Kathleen asked, "Well, what now? Do we continue working in sweatshops, being walked home at night by cops like Officer Patrick who turned on us the minute we struck, living in that Wooster Street rathole, getting nowhere?"

They walked uptown in silence, eventually finding themselves in the park.

"We have to continue working where we are, for now," Rose said, "and living where we are and like we do. For a while at least. We have no money. Less since we came here today instead of going to work."

"We've saved twenty-three dollars since you moved in."

"Not much to show for ten months' work, is it?"

"If we could save five hundred dollars we'd be able to move on, get better jobs, live in a better place." Kathleen tried to sound enthusiastic.

"And then the money runs out, and we end up back in these dumps."

Kathleen sat on a bench and huddled into herself. "I've been thinking."

"We're in trouble." They laughed lightly at Rose's silly remark.

"You could go to college."

Now Rose really laughed. "And do what?"

"What do you want to do?"

Rose laughed again, but not as hard this time. "I can't imagine. I've never thought about going to school. I've never been to school. Me mam taught me to read and write. She was a stickler about that all right, but I don't do much, meself."

"I know what you could do."

Rose draped an arm across the back of the bench and moved closer to Kathleen. A man and woman passed by. The woman whose hand he held so easily deliberately gazed toward the arch. The man glared at Kathleen and Rose. They, in turn, glowered back at him. He finally glanced away, his brow angrily furrowed.

"Son of a bitch," Rose muttered. "I know what he knows, and I know how to do it better."

Kathleen smiled and moved closer to Rose. The wind was becoming brisk. She breathed deeply of the fresh air. "Yes," she said. "You can." She watched a gray squirrel make his way across a snowy branch high in the air. "I know what you could study in college," Kathleen said, bringing them back to their discussion.

"Now why am I not a bit surprised that you've had thoughts about that, too?"

Kathleen leaned forward, propping her elbows on her knees, resting her cheeks between her hands. "I think a lot at my sewing machine. There was a time all I could think about was the machine. I was stabbed clear through my fingers six times by the needle before I learned to really pay attention. But I can drift now and never get stabbed. It gives me lots of time to think about important things. Very important things." She sat up again. "Like what you should learn about."

"And what would that be, Miss Thoughtful."

"I'm serious, and you're making fun."

"Then tell me."

"We hate the sweatshop system. We hate the injuries, the deaths. Conditions aren't that much better and probably never will be. Thirty years from now, maybe fifty, not much will have changed for the worker. We need fighters. You're a fighter, Rose.

You've always been a fighter. You could go to school and learn to fight. Fight like Max Steuer did. He got Harris and Blanck off, and I think they were guilty as hell."

Rose growled, "Steuer got off two men who should hang. Those men and women didn't need to die. I don't want to be freeing people like that. I wouldn't want to study the law and end up like that." Rose removed her arm from the back of the bench and clutched her hands together. "Murderers, that's how I see them."

"I don't want you doing that either. You'd study for the rights of the working people, not for management. Good heavens, you're such a reactionary."

Rose looked with surprise at Kathleen. "God, listen to you. You already sound like a lawyer." She fell silent, thoughtful. "Yes, you do. Yes . . ." She stood and began pacing before Kathleen. "Yes, it could work. It really could work. You're educated, aren't you? Didn't you tell me once that you taught school in Ireland?"

"I did," Kathleen said.

"Well, I don't have any education. I'd have a lot of work to do before I could even begin. But you, Kathleen darling, you could begin now. Or soon anyway, as soon as we saved a little more money."

Kathleen leaped up. "No, Rose. You're older, wiser. You jumped right into the union. You know much more about it than I do. You should go. The union needs you."

Rose took Kathleen's hands and led her back to the bench. "That's so, darling. I know a lot about the union. I could continue to learn and be real useful. There's lots more to be done. But I'm older, much older than you ..."

"Only twenty years."

"Twenty-one."

"It doesn't seem it."

"Aye, but it is, darling. Not as we live together, not as we make love and certainly not right now. But it'll seem it in the future." Rose again put her arm behind Kathleen and warded off an irritated male glance with one of her own. She turned her attention back to Kathleen. "You, darling, have years ahead of you. You could give many more years of lawyering to the union than I can. You should be practical about this."

"I am. And I see you as the smarter one. Not me."

"You're just daft. We're both smart."

"You're worse than I am, Rose Stewart."

"No, no, I'm not. And you're the one going to school. Not me."

"No, Rose darling. You're daft, and you're going to school." She stood and gave Rose a smart pat on the arm. "You're going, you're going." She began to run from Rose.

"I am not!" Rose yelled, trying to catch up to Kathleen who continued shouting over her shoulder, "You're crazy, and you're going."

Several people stopped to watch the two adults running through the park, shouting and laughing, scooping up snow and throwing it at each other.

Kathleen darted behind a tree just in time to avoid getting hit by a large snowball. They had not decided who would go to school, but it was sure one

232

of them would . . . maybe the one who won this snowball fight. Kathleen threw a ball with all her might, just skimming Rose's coat.

Meanwhile, they would continue working in the hated sweatshop, live in the depressing apartment, scrimping and saving and doing all they could to fight for the union's causes. They would do it together, sometimes laughing, sometimes crying and sometimes arguing like hell because the load was so awful for them both.

"But we'll do it, by God," Kathleen said. "We'll do it."

Her mind had drifted. She was not paying attention, and a snowball hit her smack dab in the middle of her forehead as she peeked out from behind the tree.

Scraping away the snow, she said, "By all the blessed saints, Rose Stewart, now there *is* going to be a fight!"

A few of the publications of
THE NAIAD PRESS, INC.
P.O. Box 10543 • Tallahassee, Florida 32302
Phone (904) 539-5965
Toll-Free Order Number: 1-800-533-1973
Mail orders welcome. Please include 15% postage.

SMOKEY O by Celia Cohen. 176 pp. Relationships on the playing field.   ISBN 1-56280-057-4 $9.95

KATHLEEN O'DONALD by Penny Hayes. 256 pp. Rose and Kathleen find each other and employment in 1909 NYC.
ISBN 1-56280-070-1   9.95

STAYING HOME by Elisabeth Nonas. 256 pp. Molly and Alix want a baby . . . or do they?   ISBN 1-56280-076-0   10.95

TRUE LOVE by Jennifer Fulton. 240 pp. Six lesbians searching for love in all the "right" places.   ISBN 1-56280-035-3   9.95

GARDENIAS WHERE THERE ARE NONE by Molleen Zanger. 176 pp. Why is Melanie inextricably drawn to the old house?
ISBN 1-56280-056-6   9.95

MICHAELA by Sarah Aldridge. 256 pp. A "Sarah Aldridge" romance.   ISBN 1-56280-055-8   10.95

KEEPING SECRETS by Penny Mickelbury. 208 pp. A Gianna Maglione Mystery. First in a series.   ISBN 1-56280-052-3   9.95

THE ROMANTIC NAIAD edited by Katherine V. Forrest & Barbara Grier. 336 pp. Love stories by Naiad Press women.
ISBN 1-56280-054-X   14.95

UNDER MY SKIN by Jaye Maiman. 336 pp. A Robin Miller mystery. 3rd in a series.   ISBN 1-56280-049-3.   10.95

STAY TOONED by Rhonda Dicksion. 144 pp. Cartoons — 1st collection since *Lesbian Survival Manual.*   ISBN 1-56280-045-0   9.95

CAR POOL by Karin Kallmaker. 272pp. Lesbians on wheels and then some!   ISBN 1-56280-048-5   9.95

NOT TELLING MOTHER: STORIES FROM A LIFE by Diane Salvatore. 176 pp. Her 3rd novel.   ISBN 1-56280-044-2   9.95

GOBLIN MARKET by Lauren Wright Douglas. 240pp. A Caitlin Reece Mystery. 5th in a series.   ISBN 1-56280-047-7   9.95

LONG GOODBYES by Nikki Baker. 256 pp. A Virginia Kelly mystery. 3rd in a series.   ISBN 1-56280-042-6   9.95

FRIENDS AND LOVERS by Jackie Calhoun. 224 pp. Mid-western
Lesbian lives and loves.   ISBN 1-56280-041-8   9.95

THE CAT CAME BACK by Hilary Mullins. 208 pp. Highly praised
Lesbian novel.   ISBN 1-56280-040-X   9.95

BEHIND CLOSED DOORS by Robbi Sommers. 192 pp. Hot, erotic
short stories.   ISBN 1-56280-039-6   9.95

CLAIRE OF THE MOON by Nicole Conn. 192 pp. See the movie —
read the book!   ISBN 1-56280-038-8   10.95

SILENT HEART by Claire McNab. 192 pp. Exotic Lesbian
romance.   ISBN 1-56280-036-1   9.95

HAPPY ENDINGS by Kate Brandt. 272 pp. Intimate conversations
with Lesbian authors.   ISBN 1-56280-050-7   10.95

THE SPY IN QUESTION by Amanda Kyle Williams. 256 pp. 4th
Madison McGuire.   ISBN 1-56280-037-X   9.95

SAVING GRACE by Jennifer Fulton. 240 pp. Adventure and
romantic entanglement.   ISBN 1-56280-051-5   9.95

THE YEAR SEVEN by Molleen Zanger. 208 pp. Women surviving
in a new world.   ISBN 1-56280-034-5   9.95

CURIOUS WINE by Katherine V. Forrest. 176 pp. Tenth
Anniversary Edition. The most popular contemporary Lesbian
love story.   ISBN 1-56280-053-1   9.95

CHAUTAUQUA by Catherine Ennis. 192 pp. Exciting, romantic
adventure.   ISBN 1-56280-032-9   9.95

A PROPER BURIAL by Pat Welch. 192 pp. A Helen Black
mystery. 3rd in a series.   ISBN 1-56280-033-7   9.95

SILVERLAKE HEAT: A Novel of Suspense by Carol Schmidt.
240 pp. Rhonda is as hot as Laney's dreams.   ISBN 1-56280-031-0   9.95

LOVE, ZENA BETH by Diane Salvatore. 224 pp. The most talked
about lesbian novel of the nineties!   ISBN 1-56280-030-2   9.95

A DOORYARD FULL OF FLOWERS by Isabel Miller. 160 pp.
Stories incl. 2 sequels to *Patience and Sarah*.   ISBN 1-56280-029-9   9.95

MURDER BY TRADITION by Katherine V. Forrest. 288 pp. A
Kate Delafield Mystery. 4th in a series.   ISBN 1-56280-002-7   9.95

THE EROTIC NAIAD edited by Katherine V. Forrest & Barbara Grier.
224 pp. Love stories by Naiad Press authors.   ISBN 1-56280-026-4   12.95

DEAD CERTAIN by Claire McNab. 224 pp. A Carol Ashton
mystery. 5th in a series.   ISBN 1-56280-027-2   9.95

CRAZY FOR LOVING by Jaye Maiman. 320 pp. A Robin Miller
mystery. 2nd in a series.   ISBN 1-56280-025-6   9.95

STONEHURST by Barbara Johnson. 176 pp. Passionate regency
romance.   ISBN 1-56280-024-8   9.95

INTRODUCING AMANDA VALENTINE by Rose Beecham.
256 pp. An Amanda Valentine Mystery. First in a series.
ISBN 1-56280-021-3   9.95

UNCERTAIN COMPANIONS by Robbi Sommers. 204 pp.
Steamy, erotic novel.   ISBN 1-56280-017-5   9.95

A TIGER'S HEART by Lauren W. Douglas. 240 pp. A Caitlin
Reece mystery. 4th in a series.   ISBN 1-56280-018-3   9.95

PAPERBACK ROMANCE by Karin Kallmaker. 256 pp. A
delicious romance.   ISBN 1-56280-019-1   9.95

MORTON RIVER VALLEY by Lee Lynch. 304 pp. Lee Lynch at
her best!   ISBN 1-56280-016-7   9.95

THE LAVENDER HOUSE MURDER by Nikki Baker. 224 pp. A
Virginia Kelly Mystery. 2nd in a series.   ISBN 1-56280-012-4   9.95

PASSION BAY by Jennifer Fulton. 224 pp. Passionate romance,
virgin beaches, tropical skies.   ISBN 1-56280-028-0   9.95

STICKS AND STONES by Jackie Calhoun. 208 pp. Contemporary
lesbian lives and loves.   ISBN 1-56280-020-5   9.95

DELIA IRONFOOT by Jeane Harris. 192 pp. Adventure for Delia
and Beth in the Utah mountains.   ISBN 1-56280-014-0   9.95

UNDER THE SOUTHERN CROSS by Claire McNab. 192 pp.
Romantic nights Down Under.   ISBN 1-56280-011-6   9.95

RIVERFINGER WOMEN by Elana Nachman/Dykewomon.
208 pp. Classic Lesbian/feminist novel.   ISBN 1-56280-013-2   8.95

A CERTAIN DISCONTENT by Cleve Boutell. 240 pp. A unique
coterie of women.   ISBN 1-56280-009-4   9.95

GRASSY FLATS by Penny Hayes. 256 pp. Lesbian romance in
the '30s.   ISBN 1-56280-010-8   9.95

A SINGULAR SPY by Amanda K. Williams. 192 pp. 3rd Madison
McGuire.   ISBN 1-56280-008-6   8.95

THE END OF APRIL by Penny Sumner. 240 pp. A Victoria Cross
Mystery. First in a series.   ISBN 1-56280-007-8   8.95

A FLIGHT OF ANGELS by Sarah Aldridge. 240 pp. Romance set at
the National Gallery of Art   ISBN 1-56280-001-9   9.95

HOUSTON TOWN by Deborah Powell. 208 pp. A Hollis Carpenter
mystery. Second in a series.   ISBN 1-56280-006-X   8.95

KISS AND TELL by Robbi Sommers. 192 pp. Scorching stories by
the author of *Pleasures.*   ISBN 1-56280-005-1   9.95

STILL WATERS by Pat Welch. 208 pp. A Helen Black mystery.
2nd in a series.   ISBN 0-941483-97-5   9.95

TO LOVE AGAIN by Evelyn Kennedy. 208 pp. Wildly
romantic love story.   ISBN 0-941483-85-1   9.95

IN THE GAME by Nikki Baker. 192 pp. A Virginia Kelly
mystery. First in a series.   ISBN 1-56280-004-3   9.95

AVALON by Mary Jane Jones. 256 pp. A Lesbian Arthurian
romance.   ISBN 0-941483-96-7   9.95

STRANDED by Camarin Grae. 320 pp. Entertaining, riveting
adventure.   ISBN 0-941483-99-1   9.95

THE DAUGHTERS OF ARTEMIS by Lauren Wright Douglas.
240 pp. A Caitlin Reece mystery. 3rd in a series.
                                               ISBN 0-941483-95-9   9.95

CLEARWATER by Catherine Ennis. 176 pp. Romantic secrets
of a small Louisiana town.   ISBN 0-941483-65-7   8.95

THE HALLELUJAH MURDERS by Dorothy Tell. 176 pp. A Poppy
Dillworth mystery. 2nd in a series.   ISBN 0-941483-88-6   8.95

ZETA BASE by Judith Alguire. 208 pp. Lesbian triangle
on a future Earth.   ISBN 0-941483-94-0   9.95

SECOND CHANCE by Jackie Calhoun. 256 pp. Contemporary
Lesbian lives and loves.   ISBN 0-941483-93-2   9.95

BENEDICTION by Diane Salvatore. 272 pp. Striking,
contemporary romantic novel.   ISBN 0-941483-90-8   9.95

CALLING RAIN by Karen Marie Christa Minns. 240 pp.
Spellbinding, erotic love story   ISBN 0-941483-87-8   9.95

BLACK IRIS by Jeane Harris. 192 pp. Caroline's hidden past . . .
                                               ISBN 0-941483-68-1   8.95

TOUCHWOOD by Karin Kallmaker. 240 pp. Loving, May/
December romance.   ISBN 0-941483-76-2   9.95

BAYOU CITY SECRETS by Deborah Powell. 224 pp. A Hollis
Carpenter mystery. First in a series.   ISBN 0-941483-91-6   9.95

COP OUT by Claire McNab. 208 pp. A Carol Ashton mystery.
4th in a series.   ISBN 0-941483-84-3   9.95

LODESTAR by Phyllis Horn. 224 pp. Romantic, fast-moving
adventure.   ISBN 0-941483-83-5   8.95

THE BEVERLY MALIBU by Katherine V. Forrest. 288 pp. A
Kate Delafield Mystery. 3rd in a series.   ISBN 0-941483-48-7   9.95

THAT OLD STUDEBAKER by Lee Lynch. 272 pp. Andy's affair
with Regina and her attachment to her beloved car.
                                               ISBN 0-941483-82-7   9.95

PASSION'S LEGACY by Lori Paige. 224 pp. Sarah is swept into
the arms of Augusta Pym in this delightful historical romance.
                                               ISBN 0-941483-81-9   8.95

THE PROVIDENCE FILE by Amanda Kyle Williams. 256 pp.
Second Madison McGuire   ISBN 0-941483-92-4   8.95

I LEFT MY HEART by Jaye Maiman. 320 pp. A Robin Miller
Mystery. First in a series.   ISBN 0-941483-72-X   9.95

THE PRICE OF SALT by Patricia Highsmith (writing as Claire
Morgan). 288 pp. Classic lesbian novel, first issued in 1952 . . .
acknowledged by its author under her own, very famous, name.
                                           ISBN 1-56280-003-5   9.95

SIDE BY SIDE by Isabel Miller. 256 pp. From beloved author of
Patience and Sarah.   ISBN 0-941483-77-0   9.95

STAYING POWER: LONG TERM LESBIAN COUPLES
by Susan E. Johnson. 352 pp. Joys of coupledom.
                                           ISBN 0-941-483-75-4   12.95

SLICK by Camarin Grae. 304 pp. Exotic, erotic adventure.
                                           ISBN 0-941483-74-6   9.95

NINTH LIFE by Lauren Wright Douglas. 256 pp. A Caitlin
Reece mystery. 2nd in a series.   ISBN 0-941483-50-9   8.95

PLAYERS by Robbi Sommers. 192 pp. Sizzling, erotic novel.
                                           ISBN 0-941483-73-8   9.95

MURDER AT RED ROOK RANCH by Dorothy Tell. 224 pp.
A Poppy Dillworth mystery. 1st in a series.   ISBN 0-941483-80-0   8.95

LESBIAN SURVIVAL MANUAL by Rhonda Dicksion.
112 pp. Cartoons!   ISBN 0-941483-71-1   8.95

A ROOM FULL OF WOMEN by Elisabeth Nonas. 256 pp.
Contemporary Lesbian lives.   ISBN 0-941483-69-X   9.95

PRIORITIES by Lynda Lyons 288 pp. Science fiction with
a twist.   ISBN 0-941483-66-5   8.95

THEME FOR DIVERSE INSTRUMENTS by Jane Rule. 208
pp. Powerful romantic lesbian stories.   ISBN 0-941483-63-0   8.95

LESBIAN QUERIES by Hertz & Ertman. 112 pp. The questions
you were too embarrassed to ask.   ISBN 0-941483-67-3   8.95

CLUB 12 by Amanda Kyle Williams. 288 pp. Espionage thriller
featuring a lesbian agent!   ISBN 0-941483-64-9   8.95

DEATH DOWN UNDER by Claire McNab. 240 pp. A Carol
Ashton mystery. 3rd in a series.   ISBN 0-941483-39-8   9.95

MONTANA FEATHERS by Penny Hayes. 256 pp. Vivian and
Elizabeth find love in frontier Montana.   ISBN 0-941483-61-4   8.95

CHESAPEAKE PROJECT by Phyllis Horn. 304 pp. Jessie &
Meredith in perilous adventure.   ISBN 0-941483-58-4   8.95

LIFESTYLES by Jackie Calhoun. 224 pp. Contemporary Lesbian
lives and loves.   ISBN 0-941483-57-6   9.95

VIRAGO by Karen Marie Christa Minns. 208 pp. Darsen has
chosen Ginny.   ISBN 0-941483-56-8   8.95

WILDERNESS TREK by Dorothy Tell. 192 pp. Six women on
vacation learning "new" skills.   ISBN 0-941483-60-6   8.95

MURDER BY THE BOOK by Pat Welch. 256 pp. A Helen
Black Mystery. First in a series.   ISBN 0-941483-59-2   9.95

LESBIANS IN GERMANY by Lillian Faderman & B. Eriksson.
128 pp. Fiction, poetry, essays.   ISBN 0-941483-62-2   8.95

THERE'S SOMETHING I'VE BEEN MEANING TO TELL
YOU Ed. by Loralee MacPike. 288 pp. Gay men and lesbians
coming out to their children.   ISBN 0-941483-44-4   9.95

LIFTING BELLY by Gertrude Stein. Ed. by Rebecca Mark. 104
pp. Erotic poetry.   ISBN 0-941483-51-7   8.95

ROSE PENSKI by Roz Perry. 192 pp. Adult lovers in a long-term
relationship.   ISBN 0-941483-37-1   8.95

AFTER THE FIRE by Jane Rule. 256 pp. Warm, human novel
by this incomparable author.   ISBN 0-941483-45-2   8.95

SUE SLATE, PRIVATE EYE by Lee Lynch. 176 pp. The gay
folk of Peacock Alley are *all cats*.   ISBN 0-941483-52-5   8.95

CHRIS by Randy Salem. 224 pp. Golden oldie. Handsome Chris
and her adventures.   ISBN 0-941483-42-8   8.95

THREE WOMEN by March Hastings. 232 pp. Golden oldie. A
triangle among wealthy sophisticates.   ISBN 0-941483-43-6   8.95

RICE AND BEANS by Valeria Taylor. 232 pp. Love and
romance on poverty row.   ISBN 0-941483-41-X   8.95

PLEASURES by Robbi Sommers. 204 pp. Unprecedented
eroticism.   ISBN 0-941483-49-5   8.95

EDGEWISE by Camarin Grae. 372 pp. Spellbinding
adventure.   ISBN 0-941483-19-3   9.95

FATAL REUNION by Claire McNab. 224 pp. A Carol Ashton
mystery. 2nd in a series.   ISBN 0-941483-40-1   8.95

KEEP TO ME STRANGER by Sarah Aldridge. 372 pp. Romance
set in a department store dynasty.   ISBN 0-941483-38-X   9.95

IN THE BLOOD by Lauren Wright Douglas. 252 pp. Lesbian
science fiction adventure fantasy   ISBN 0-941483-22-3   8.95

THE BEE'S KISS by Shirley Verel. 216 pp. Delicate, delicious
romance.   ISBN 0-941483-36-3   8.95

RAGING MOTHER MOUNTAIN by Pat Emmerson. 264 pp.
Furosa Firechild's adventures in Wonderland.   ISBN 0-941483-35-5   8.95

IN EVERY PORT by Karin Kallmaker. 228 pp. Jessica's sexy,
adventuresome travels.   ISBN 0-941483-37-7   9.95

OF LOVE AND GLORY by Evelyn Kennedy. 192 pp. Exciting
WWII romance. ISBN 0-941483-32-0   8.95

CLICKING STONES by Nancy Tyler Glenn. 288 pp. Love
transcending time. ISBN 0-941483-31-2   9.95

SURVIVING SISTERS by Gail Pass. 252 pp. Powerful love
story. ISBN 0-941483-16-9   8.95

SOUTH OF THE LINE by Catherine Ennis. 216 pp. Civil War
adventure. ISBN 0-941483-29-0   8.95

WOMAN PLUS WOMAN by Dolores Klaich. 300 pp. Supurb
Lesbian overview. ISBN 0-941483-28-2   9.95

HEAVY GILT by Delores Klaich. 192 pp. Lesbian detective/
disappearing homophobes/upper class gay society.

ISBN 0-941483-25-8   8.95

THE FINER GRAIN by Denise Ohio. 216 pp. Brilliant young
college lesbian novel. ISBN 0-941483-11-8   8.95

HIGH CONTRAST by Jessie Lattimore. 264 pp. Women of the
Crystal Palace. ISBN 0-941483-17-7   8.95

OCTOBER OBSESSION by Meredith More. Josie's rich, secret
Lesbian life. ISBN 0-941483-18-5   8.95

BEFORE STONEWALL: THE MAKING OF A GAY AND
LESBIAN COMMUNITY by Andrea Weiss & Greta Schiller.
96 pp., 25 illus. ISBN 0-941483-20-7   7.95

WE WALK THE BACK OF THE TIGER by Patricia A. Murphy.
192 pp. Romantic Lesbian novel/beginning women's movement.
ISBN 0-941483-13-4   8.95

SUNDAY'S CHILD by Joyce Bright. 216 pp. Lesbian athletics, at
last the novel about sports. ISBN 0-941483-12-6   8.95

OSTEN'S BAY by Zenobia N. Vole. 204 pp. Sizzling adventure
romance set on Bonaire. ISBN 0-941483-15-0   8.95

LESSONS IN MURDER by Claire McNab. 216 pp. A Carol
Ashton mystery. First in a series. ISBN 0-941483-14-2   9.95

YELLOWTHROAT by Penny Hayes. 240 pp. Margarita, bandit,
kidnaps Julia. ISBN 0-941483-10-X   8.95

SAPPHISTRY: THE BOOK OF LESBIAN SEXUALITY by
Pat Califia. 3d edition, revised. 208 pp. ISBN 0-941483-24-X   10.95

CHERISHED LOVE by Evelyn Kennedy. 192 pp. Erotic
Lesbian love story. ISBN 0-941483-08-8   9.95

LAST SEPTEMBER by Helen R. Hull. 208 pp. Six stories & a
glorious novella. ISBN 0-941483-09-6   8.95

THE SECRET IN THE BIRD by Camarin Grae. 312 pp. Striking,
psychological suspense novel. ISBN 0-941483-05-3   8.95

SURPLUS by Sylvia Stevenson. 342 pp. A classic early Lesbian
novel.   ISBN 0-930044-78-9   7.95

PEMBROKE PARK by Michelle Martin. 256 pp. Derring-do
and daring romance in Regency England.   ISBN 0-930044-77-0   7.95

THE LONG TRAIL by Penny Hayes. 248 pp. Vivid adventures
of two women in love in the old west.   ISBN 0-930044-76-2   8.95

AN EMERGENCE OF GREEN by Katherine V. Forrest. 288
pp. Powerful novel of sexual discovery.   ISBN 0-930044-69-X   9.95

THE LESBIAN PERIODICALS INDEX edited by Claire
Potter. 432 pp. Author & subject index.   ISBN 0-930044-74-6   12.95

DESERT OF THE HEART by Jane Rule. 224 pp. A classic;
basis for the movie *Desert Hearts*.   ISBN 0-930044-73-8   9.95

FOR KEEPS by Elisabeth Nonas. 144 pp. Contemporary novel
about losing and finding love.   ISBN 0-930044-71-1   7.95

TORCHLIGHT TO VALHALLA by Gale Wilhelm. 128 pp.
Classic novel by a great Lesbian writer.   ISBN 0-930044-68-1   7.95

LESBIAN NUNS: BREAKING SILENCE edited by Rosemary
Curb and Nancy Manahan. 432 pp. Unprecedented autobiographies
of religious life.   ISBN 0-930044-62-2   9.95

THE SWASHBUCKLER by Lee Lynch. 288 pp. Colorful novel
set in Greenwich Village in the sixties.   ISBN 0-930044-66-5   8.95

MISFORTUNE'S FRIEND by Sarah Aldridge. 320 pp. Historical Lesbian novel set on two continents.   ISBN 0-930044-67-3   7.95

SEX VARIANT WOMEN IN LITERATURE by Jeannette
Howard Foster. 448 pp. Literary history.   ISBN 0-930044-65-7   8.95

A HOT-EYED MODERATE by Jane Rule. 252 pp. Hard-hitting
essays on gay life; writing; art.   ISBN 0-930044-57-6   7.95

WE TOO ARE DRIFTING by Gale Wilhelm. 128 pp. Timeless
Lesbian novel, a masterpiece.   ISBN 0-930044-61-4   6.95

AMATEUR CITY by Katherine V. Forrest. 224 pp. A Kate
Delafield mystery. First in a series.   ISBN 0-930044-55-X   9.95

THE SOPHIE HOROWITZ STORY by Sarah Schulman. 176
pp. Engaging novel of madcap intrigue.   ISBN 0-930044-54-1   7.95

THE YOUNG IN ONE ANOTHER'S ARMS by Jane Rule.
224 pp. Classic Jane Rule.   ISBN 0-930044-53-3   9.95

OLD DYKE TALES by Lee Lynch. 224 pp. Extraordinary
stories of our diverse Lesbian lives.   ISBN 0-930044-51-7   8.95

DAUGHTERS OF A CORAL DAWN by Katherine V. Forrest.
240 pp. Novel set in a Lesbian new world.   ISBN 0-930044-50-9   9.95

AGAINST THE SEASON by Jane Rule. 224 pp. Luminous,
complex novel of interrelationships.   ISBN 0-930044-48-7   8.95

LOVERS IN THE PRESENT AFTERNOON by Kathleen
Fleming. 288 pp. A novel about recovery and growth.
                              ISBN 0-930044-46-0   8.95

TOOTHPICK HOUSE by Lee Lynch. 264 pp. Love between
two Lesbians of different classes.   ISBN 0-930044-45-2   7.95

MADAME AURORA by Sarah Aldridge. 256 pp. Historical
novel featuring a charismatic "seer."   ISBN 0-930044-44-4   7.95

CONTRACT WITH THE WORLD by Jane Rule. 340 pp.
Powerful, panoramic novel of gay life.   ISBN 0-930044-28-2   9.95

THE NESTING PLACE by Sarah Aldridge. 224 pp. A
three-woman triangle — love conquers all!   ISBN 0-930044-26-6   7.95

THIS IS NOT FOR YOU by Jane Rule. 284 pp. A letter to a
beloved is also an intricate novel.   ISBN 0-930044-25-8   8.95

ANNA'S COUNTRY by Elizabeth Lang. 208 pp. A woman
finds her Lesbian identity.   ISBN 0-930044-19-3   8.95

PRISM by Valerie Taylor. 158 pp. A love affair between two
women in their sixties.   ISBN 0-930044-18-5   6.95

OUTLANDER by Jane Rule. 207 pp. Short stories and essays
by one of our finest writers.   ISBN 0-930044-17-7   8.95

ALL TRUE LOVERS by Sarah Aldridge. 292 pp. Romantic
novel set in the 1930s and 1940s.   ISBN 0-930044-10-X   8.95

CYTHEREA'S BREATH by Sarah Aldridge. 240 pp. Romantic
novel about women's entrance into medicine.
                              ISBN 0-930044-02-9   6.95

TOTTIE by Sarah Aldridge. 181 pp. Lesbian romance in the
turmoil of the sixties.   ISBN 0-930044-01-0   6.95

THE LATECOMER by Sarah Aldridge. 107 pp. A delicate love
story.   ISBN 0-930044-00-2   6.95

ODD GIRL OUT by Ann Bannon.   ISBN 0-930044-83-5   5.95
I AM A WOMAN 84-3; WOMEN IN THE SHADOWS 85-1;   each
JOURNEY TO A WOMAN 86-X; BEEBO BRINKER 87-8. Golden
oldies about life in Greenwich Village.

JOURNEY TO FULFILLMENT, A WORLD WITHOUT MEN, and   3.95
RETURN TO LESBOS. All by Valerie Taylor   each

These are just a few of the many Naiad Press titles — we are the oldest and
largest lesbian/feminist publishing company in the world. Please request a
complete catalog. We offer personal service; we encourage and welcome direct
mail orders from individuals who have limited access to bookstores carrying
our publications.